THE MUSLIM PRINCE

What if Diana hadn't died?

Roger Ley

H. Deana + her
prediliction for
brown boys!!..
Roger Ley + I used to
go to Tom Corbett's writing
group!

Copyright

The Muslim Prince

Copyright © 2019 by Roger Ley. All Rights Reserved.

Cover design Roger Ley

Cover image Ioana Radu courtesy of Pixabay

This book is a work of fiction. Names, characters, places and
incidents either are products of the author's imagination
or are used fictitiously. Any resemblance to actual persons,
living or dead, events or locales is entirely coincidental.

Roger Ley

Visit my website at rogerley.co.uk

First Printing: 2019

rev 2

For Dodi and Diana

'*Dead yesterdays and unborn tomorrows, why fret about them if today is sweet.*'

OMAR KHAYYAM

'*The past is the price we pay for the present.*'

ALAN JUDD

'*There is no such thing as destiny, there are only different choices*'

WALTER SPARROW, FILM 'THE NUMBER 23'

*A list of characters and a glossary of
Arabic words and phrases appears
at the end of the book*

CONTENTS

PROLOGUE

Ritz Hotel, Paris 1997

In the staff changing room Dodi Fayed's driver, Henri Paul, knelt, copiously throwing up into the toilet pan. A bodyguard stood watching indifferently. He phoned Dodi's Head of Security.

'He isn't fit to drive DnD, Boss,' he said. With grim humour, he held the phone near to Henri's head as he began another noisy episode, then brought it back up to his ear.

'Okay, okay, get somebody else to drive,' said his boss. 'Give it to Marcos: he's careful. Tell him to bring the car round to the back now, they're ready to leave.' The bodyguard left Henri Paul to his misery and went to find Marcos. As he passed the front desk, he told the receptionist about Henri Paul. *A problem delegated is a problem solved,* he thought. Henri was their concern now, and anyway, he was paid to hurt people, when necessary, not to nurse them.

Security guards escorted Diana and Dodi to the black Mercedes S280 as it arrived at the rear of the hotel. Dodi followed Diana into the back seat. Marcos felt surprisingly calm at the prospect of driving two of the world's most well-known celebrities. As an ex-police driver, he knew the streets of Paris intimately; he had driven many of them at speed on numerous occasions and wasn't going to be intimidated by the paparazzi waiting outside with their shoulder cams and loudly revving motorcycles. He would drive fast but within the limits of his training and experience. Before he let out the clutch, he looked into the rear-view mirror and spoke to his passengers on the back seat.

'Monsieur, Madam, please fasten your seat belts.'

Dodi and Diana glanced at each other as if surprised at his presumption but then complied.

The Wedding of Prince William and Isabella Calthorpe

From Wikipedia, the free encyclopaedia

The wedding of Prince William and Isabella Calthorpe took place on 30 April 2010 at Westminster Abbey in London, United Kingdom. The groom, Prince William is second in the line of succession to the British Throne. He and the bride, Isabella Calthorpe, have been close friends since 2004.

The Dean of Westminster, John Hall, presided at the service. The Archbishop of Canterbury, Rowan Williams, conducted the marriage. Richard Chartres, the Bishop of London, preached the sermon. A reading was given by the bride's brother Jacobi. William's best man was his brother, Prince Harry, while the bride's sister Gabriella, was the maid of honour. The ceremony was attended by family members from both sides, as well as by senior members of a number of foreign royal families, diplomats, and the couple's chosen personal guests. After the ceremony, the couple made the traditional appearance on the royal balcony of Buckingham Palace.

Prince William and Isabella met in 2002. Their

engagement on 21 October 2009 was announced on 17th November 2009. The build-up to the wedding and the occasion itself attracted much media attention, being compared in many ways to the 1981 marriage of William's parents, Prince Charles and Lady Diana Spencer. The occasion was a public holiday in the United Kingdom and featured many ceremonial aspects, including state carriages and roles for the Foot Guards and House-hold Cavalry.

Prince James of Cambridge

From Wikipedia, the free encyclopaedia

Prince James of Cambridge (James Henry Richard; born 16th February 2013) is a member of the British royal family. He is the eldest son of Prince William, Duke of Cambridge, and Isabella, Duchess of Cambridge, and is third in the line of succession to the British throne, behind his grandfather Prince Charles and his father Prince William. As he is expected to be King at some time in the future, his birth was widely celebrated across the Commonwealth. James occasionally accompanies his parents on royal tours, and is reported to have close ties with his grandmother, Diana Princess of

Wales, and his step-grandfather, Dodi Fayed.

CHAPTER 1

Throughout his childhood, James had enjoyed time spent with his relatives, the Fayeds, on their country estate at Oxted. James loved the long flowing clothes and colourful scarves that the women wore, the unusual food that was served and the melodious sounding language they used. The Muslim half of his family was so much more interesting and exotic than the Windsors, who carried their history like a wet greatcoat. His Uncle Faisil and Aunt Aisha were about fifteen years older than him but they called each other cousins. Faisil, who was famous for his sense of humour, took a great interest in his nephew, James.

It was Ramadan, and the Spring weather was cool enough to merit a log fire in the hearth of the large living room. As the evening light dimmed, the whole family sat cross-legged on thick carpets strewn with colourful cushions. As an experiment, James hadn't eaten or drunk all day and was looking forward to the *iftar*, the first meal after the day's fast. His younger sister, Victoria, had been given snacks, out of sight, in the kitchen.

The sun had set and they sat circled around a large linen cloth. *Hadj* Dodi consulted his watch and after a short pause clapped his hands. Servants bustled in with plates of rice, vegetables, salads and meat. The family began to help themselves, trying not to seem too eager even though they were famished.

Uncle Faisil offered a small dish of dates to Victoria, 'Sheep's eyeballs, *Habibi*?' he asked innocently and laughed as she pulled a face and turned her head. Victoria was less adventurous than her brother James when it came to food.

He offered them to James and, using a stage Yorkshire accent, said, 'Remember to eat with your right hand, Lad.' The whole family laughed as they remembered the first time he was told this, several years earlier. He had made the mistake of asking why, and Faisil had whispered the explanation, much to the amusement of his sister Aisha. Diana and Hadj Dodi had pretended not to hear and carried on eating. James blushed at the memory.

'I'll never be allowed to forget that, will I?' he said ruefully. Everybody laughed except James and the Hadj.

On occasions like this Hadj Dodi, now in his late sixties, liked to wear his red prayer hat. He enjoyed 'instructing' his step-grandson, and James would play up to this by asking questions he and Faisil had prepared.

'When they were travelling in the mountains during Ramadan, how did the Bedouin know what time the sun had set?' James asked the Hadj.

'They looked at their watches,' said Faisil.

'Duh,' said Victoria, enjoying a rare opportunity to put one over on her brother.

'No, no, I mean in the olden days before they had watches, Hadji.'

'Ah,' said the Hadj, pleased at the question. He passed James a choice piece from a plate of goat kabsa. Leaning back he continued, 'They compared a black thread and a white thread, and when they could no longer tell them apart, then they knew the sun had set.'

'What an elegant solution,' said Diana pretending she hadn't heard the explanation several times before.

They all carried on eating and talking until James asked a more serious question. 'What is the real difference between Islam and Christianity, Hadji? I know the prayers and services are not the same but they worship the same God.'

The Hadj considered how to make his answer simple enough for young ears. 'Well, the Christians, the Jews and the Muslims share a belief in the One God, and all three religions believe in the Scriptures. This is why we call them the "People of the Book." You could think of this belief as the trunk of a tree with three main branches.'

The family sat and listened respectfully.

'Christians believe Jesus was sent by God to save them. The Jews are still waiting for their Messiah to come and save them. Muslims believe the Koran is God's final and eternal message to humanity.'

Faisil leaned towards James and said, 'So, you pays your money and you takes your choice, Lad.' Everybody laughed, and the conversation passed to lighter topics.

***

At Vauxhall Cross, in London, the Secret Intelligence Service listeners had little to report to their political masters, apart from Dodi's continuing influence over Prince William's eldest son, James, the heir to the English throne. It was an influence that discomfited some senior members of both the Government and the Civil Service.

***

The next morning Dodi was back in European dress, wearing his jodhpurs and riding boots. James followed him out into the gardens.

'So, *Hafid*, will you come to see my birds?' Dodi asked

James was intrigued, 'What birds, Grandfather?' James called him Hadj or Grandfather depending on how occidental Dodi appeared to be feeling.

Dodi led him around the stable block to a series of large wire mesh and wooden cages containing feeders and perches. There were half a dozen of them, newly built, and each had an occupant.

'I have taken an interest in falconry, Hafid, there is a long history of it in Arabia and, coincidentally, it is a passion the English share. Not only do I enjoy the sport, but through it I have made some very useful business contacts in both London and Riyadh.'

He and James walked slowly past the cages admiring their silent occupants.

'How beautiful they are, Hafid. I love to release them and watch them soar high above me and then stoop onto their prey.' Eyes wide, Dodi used his hands to imitate the bird's flight. James could see where Faisil had inherited his sense of pantomime. 'They are doing what God created them for. What a pity we too cannot live a life as true to our instincts,' he sighed.

James nodded although, being only nine years old, he wasn't entirely sure he understood what his step-grandfather meant.

Dodi carefully opened one of the cages and they moved inside. 'Put on the glove and let the bird sit on your hand, Hafid.' He picked the bird up and offered it to James.

'What sort is it, Hadji?' asked James as the raptor sat quietly on his left hand, its head covered by a decorated leather hood.

'It is a peregrine falcon, Hafid.' He lifted the hood from the bird's head and it blinked in the watery sunlight. James felt intimidated by its hooked, grey and yellow beak but was hypnotised by the dark depths of its eyes. 'You are right to be cautious: his beak is made to slash and tear at flesh,' Dodi said as he replaced the hood and took the bird back to its perch. 'Come, Hafid, we will leave our small assassin to his murderous thoughts.'

'Can I fly it, Grandfather?'

'It is suitable for you to fly, Hafid, but not today. Another time, *inshallah*. We must get back to the house, I promised to go for a ride with Aisha.'

As they left the aviary and walked around the stables, Dodi looked over the fields and took a deep breath. 'I love the landscape of England, its growing, green dampness, but I cannot stay too long away from the desert, I yearn for its emptiness, its purity. *Al-hamdu lillah* I can spend many years in both places. It is a great shame that your grandmother abhors the desert air: she says it dries her skin. When she stays at the house in Riyadh, she looks at the servants, with their lined and leathern faces, and feels the need to rub even more cream into her own.

CHAPTER 2

Faisil, now nearly thirty, was entrusted with increasingly important business negotiations on the Hadj's behalf. He was currently representing him at a meeting with Prince Achmed bin Ahmed, a senior member of the Saudi royal family. They were negotiating the lease of land near Medina. The Hadj hoped to build inexpensive accommodation for some of the millions of the Faithful who engaged on the Holy Pilgrimage every year. The Prince had rented a room in a small hotel in the old quarter of Jeddah. It was a private and discreet establishment, which served the highest quality coffee and sweetmeats to its customers while guaranteeing comfort, solitude and discretion.

Faisil sat cross-legged on the carpeted floor and took a pull on the hookah that stood between him and Prince Achmed. He could hear the music of the oud, a short-necked lute-like instrument, played by the dwarf who had shown them to this room when they first arrived. He had an awkward gait and had, only with some difficulty, lead them up the stairs. Now he was singing quietly in the courtyard below.

Faisil didn't inhale, he wasn't a smoker and didn't want to risk having a coughing fit and make a spectacle of himself. He found the bubbling noise the contraption made rather distasteful, but this was a Saudi prince he was dealing with and business had to be conducted in the required manner. He did enjoy wearing Saudi clothing though: it was looser and more comfortable than the city suits he wore to most of his business meetings.

They began with a discussion of a range of general subjects: the health of their respective relatives, the price of oil, the current dispute between Israel and its neighbours, as well as the improprieties of various western politicians, and even the handling and performance of different four-wheel-drives in desert conditions. After the required half an hour spent on conversational niceties, the business of Dodi's lease was completed surprisingly quickly and to Faisil's satisfaction. The terms were more generous than he'd anticipated. Faisil thought the meeting was over but the Prince showed no sign of wanting to leave, instead he leaned forward, smiled and said, 'My friend, I have another matter which I wish to discuss, a matter of some delicacy.' He lifted a plate of sweetmeats and offered it to Faisil.

He wants a favour, thought Faisil, *that explains his generosity in the previous negotiation.* Faisil smiled and waited for the new subject to emerge, like the head of a turtle, which will emerge from its shell only when all seems safe.

'It is something I wish to bring to the attention of your father, Hadj Dodi, may many blessings fall upon him. Something of the greatest importance and secrecy.' The tip of the turtle's nose was just emerging.

Faisil said nothing, although his curiosity was aroused. He used the change in atmosphere as an excuse to lay down his mouthpiece.

'It concerns my father, the King,' said the Prince.

Faisil managed not to flinch in surprise. 'I am sure that my father would be happy to help the King in any way that he is able,' he said, placing his right hand over his heart. 'It would be an honour.' He felt that he might be about to swim out of his depth.

'The King desires an alliance, an alliance between the House of Saud and the House of Windsor. He thinks this a mutually advantageous enterprise for the subjects of both great countries. He hopes that your father, *inshallah*, might use his influence in this regard.'

Faisil tried to breath normally. He had not expected the meeting to take this turn. 'I see, Your Highness, er, yes, I am sure there could be great benefits for both families and, indeed, their subjects.' He'd given a neutral response while he played for time. As a diversion he picked up his mouthpiece and took a pull on the hookah. He blew out smoke and smiled, trying to put the Prince at his ease. He knew that, when dealing with these most conservative and traditional of people, a proposal must be allowed time to develop, but the turtle's head was halfway out at least.

'The King feels a marriage to be the best way of cementing this alliance,' said the Prince.

Now that Faisil could see the direction the conversation was taking; he could quantify the problem and begin to see where a profit could be made.

'A marriage between two minor members of the Families isn't impossible, Your Highness, difficult, but not impossible. It will take some research of course; we'd need to find suitable matches and then provide incentives and encouragement.'

'No, my friend, not "minor" members, the King wishes an alliance at a higher level.'

Faisil thought fast, 'Perhaps you are thinking of the children of Prince Harry and the Duchess of Sussex?'

The Prince shook his head. 'No, *Sadiki*, the King wishes the bond to be made in the direct line, he wishes his granddaughter, my daughter Malika, to marry Prince James, the heir to the English throne.'

If the turtle's head had suddenly extended and clamped itself firmly on Faisil's nose, he could not have been more surprised. 'This is a matter that I must discuss with my father and Princess Diana. Even if it were possible, it would need careful planning and great discretion.'

'It seems to the King that it would be relatively

simple to arrange such a marriage, my friend.'

'I am sorry, Prince Ahmed, but arranged royal marriages are a thing of the past in the United Kingdom. The British public will not find an arranged marriage acceptable. No, it would have appear to at least to be a love match.'

The Prince stroked his beard, and for a moment Faisil was reminded of the villain in a pantomime he had seen as a child, Ali Baba and the Forty Thieves. 'This might be more difficult to achieve,' said the Prince.

'Not necessarily,' said Faisil, 'It depends on how tractable your daughter is. How old is she?'

'She is nine years old, an intelligent girl. Her mother thinks she will be a great beauty.'

'Prince James is thirteen. We should arrange for them to meet,' said Faisil. 'A brief meeting, just so that they can begin to get to know one another. You should tell your daughter that she should be pleasant to Prince James, explain that he is an important friend of your father, the King.'

'Let us hope that we can strike a spark and then gently fan it into flames over the coming years,' said the Prince.

The meeting ended and he and Faisil walked arm in arm down the stairs to the central courtyard. They air-kissed one another on both cheeks and wished each other well, and their Families well, and hoped for the good health of the Saudi King, and the British Royal Family. The Prince left after only five minutes of these formalities. Faisil assumed he must be in a hurry, but he himself was booked on a flight back to London next morning and could relax. He sat at the edge of the fountain and listened as the dwarf sang the song of the caravan route, the *trig el bill*, the gentle ululations of his voice harmonising with the melody as he plucked the strings of his oud.

It was at times like this that he was grateful to own two languages. *Who was it said that to know another language was to have another window on the world?* he wondered. The musician transported Faisil back to the dunes, the sand, the whispering breeze, the plodding animals, the solitude:

The wind passes like a caress over the waves of the desert sand,

And the caravan leaves no more trace than a bird's wing in the air or a fish in the water.

Let us flee the crowd for in the multitude there is no salvation.

Let us beware of taking root like a tree.

The sun rises in the heavens and the feet of the camels wearily seek the shadows;

The song ended, Faisil stood, thanked the dwarf, and placed a payment on the fountain's parapet. The dwarf smiled and nodded as he began another song. Faisil walked back up the stairs to his room and his laptop. He needed to think, then he would skype Hadj Dodi. This could change the direction of his whole life. As an uncle and adviser to Prince James, the future King of England, he needed to take full advantage of the opportunities this matchmaking could offer. At the same time, he knew that this new turn of events brought great danger. The British Establishment, the palace hangers-on and the right-wing politicians would never welcome a Muslim Princess so close to the throne of England. What a wonderful way of paying them back for the slights and insults they'd heaped on his mother, Princess Diana, when she'd converted to Islam and married his father. Diana had been driven from the Royal Family after her divorce from Charles, her HRH honorific had been taken from her and she'd been ostracised by the aristocracy.

Faisil felt positively gleeful as he contacted the Hadj, and very glad that skype was encrypted.

***

The recording of the conversation between Faisil and Dodi generated a meeting of Heads of Department at the headquarters of the SIS, the Secret Intelligence Service. The upshot was a report sent to the Prime Minister via the Cabinet Secretary. A watching brief was instigated, there wasn't much else that could be done.

CHAPTER 3

Arabian Desert, Saudi Arabia: 2027

To mark his fourteenth birthday Dodi invited James to accompany him on one of his desert hunting trips. A courtier escorted him to Stansted Airport and handed him over to a flight attendant in the VIP lounge. They boarded the Fayed family Gulfstream and flew to the King Khalid airport at Riyadh where Dodi's car picked James up. It was late by the time he got to the Fayed house in the city. The Hadj welcomed him when he arrived and led him inside for a light meal before he retired.

Next morning, James was woken by the call to prayer issuing from the loudspeakers of a nearby Mosque. It was a year since his last visit and he stood on his balcony enjoying the sounds and alien smells of this very foreign city. His young senses could identify rose water, aloe, saffron, wood smoke and cooking smells that he could not yet name. He might have been on another planet, everything was different, the buildings, the vehicles, the clothes, even the street lamps. He looked forward to walking in the city where he hoped not to be recognised. There would inevitability be bodyguards, he accepted that, but he knew they would be discreet. He couldn't wait to visit the *souk*.

At breakfast, he broached an idea with the Hadj. 'If I wore local robes and a headdress when I walk in the city, I could be anybody.'

'What a good idea, Hafid, nobody will guess you are an English Prince as long as you keep your blond hair hidden.' He called for one of the house-keepers and spoke to her in Arabic. James could understand quite a lot of what was said. Dodi was ordering local clothes for him.

'Isn't there a story about Grandmother wearing a police uniform and mingling with the crowds outside Buckingham Palace, Hadj?'

Dodi snorted, 'She was very young, Hafid, and she was lucky not to have been arrested for impersonating a police officer. Now that would have been a story, "Princess Diana spends the night in a cell."' He laughed, 'Local clothing is most sensible, Hafid, it is good security, it makes perfect sense. We will make an Arab of you after all.

***

This exchange was seen as particularly concerning by the "listeners" and, after it had been transcribed, caused some animated discussion in Whitehall's corridors of power.

***

The morning was still cool. A four-by-four was

parked on the forecourt of the house. The Hadj was in a fine mood as he and James approached it. He smiled and said, 'We will sit in the back, Hafid. Mohammed will drive us, and Mufta will sit next to him looking fierce and scare away my many enemies.' Mufta was a large, silent man with a shaven head and a luxurious black moustache. He was one of Dodi's local bodyguards and had been with the family for many years. James had never seen him smile.

The Hadj wore an ankle-length white cotton robe and a red gutra headdress. James wore a khaki safari suit and a similar headdress. 'You see, Hafid, all people with even a small drop of Arab blood flowing in their veins, appreciate the beauty of the desert. The deep blue of the sky, the whisper of the sand as it flows over the dunes, driven by a wind that can suddenly conjure unearthly fingers that pull at loose clothing, an impatient djinn urging you on to the next oasis.' The Hadj gestured dramatically as he spoke, eyes wide open like a magician. James laughed, he loved it when the Hadj was in one of his poetic moods.

'Remember, Hafid, "*There is nothing in the desert, and no man needs nothing.*"'

James wasn't sure what the Hadj was telling him, but he nodded as if he understood. He looked out of the window of the car as it sped along the tarmac, the dunes and rocky outcrops passing on either side. He made a mental note to look the quotation up on the internet that evening.

Although he had not a drop of Arab blood flowing in his veins, James loved the desert. He and the Hadj travelled to their camp, miles out in the wilderness. They arrived to find that a staff of male servants had pitched a group of Bedouin-style tents. Out of sight, on the other side of a dune, they had erected a prefabricated "bloc sanitaire". The servants' quarters were behind another dune.

Mufta carried James' case to his tent, 'Check your gloves and shoes for scorpions before you put them on, *Alrajul.*' He mimicked tapping the heel of a shoe on the ground. James didn't remember being addressed by Mufta before, and to be called "Prince" was quite a surprise.'

'*Shucran*, Mufta, I will do as you say,' he said.

Mufta stamped on the ground to show him how to deal with a scorpion should such a recalcitrant beast appear. He laughed as he did so and James, was momentarily surprised by Mufta's shocking dentition. It reminded him of Stonehenge, there were as many gaps as uprights in his mouth. James now realised that it was probably embarrassment rather than Mufta's disposition that stopped him from smiling.

For two days Dodi and James flew their birds in the mornings and late afternoons, resting during the hot part of the day. James was comfortable in his tent, with rugs on the floor and a camp bed. The evenings around the campfire talking to the Hadj were his favourite time. On the morning of the third day, James and the Hadj were sitting under an awning finishing their breakfast when a large black SUV arrived at the encampment.

'Ah,' said the Hadj, 'My friend, Prince Achmed, has arrived. I asked him to come for a day's sport.' He stood up and led James out into the sun to meet him.

A servant opened the side door of the vehicle, and a tall, slim, young man wearing traditional dress alighted. '*Ahlan wa sahlan, Achmed,*' said the Hadj as he greeted his friend. He touched his right hand to his heart then embraced him and kissed him on both cheeks.

'*Ahlan biik, Hadj Dodi,*' the newcomer replied.

The Hadj introduced James and his guest to one another formally. 'Your Highness, may I present Prince James of the House of Windsor, and this, Your Highness, is Prince Achmed bin Ahmed of the House of Saud.'

James assessed Achmed as a minor prince and was unsure of the required protocol, so he gave a brief head bow and then offered his hand. Prince Achmed did the same, and everybody smiled as they shook hands. The handshake seemed to last longer than necessary, and James wondered if this was a cultural thing or perhaps there was some other significance.

Prince Achmed returned to his vehicle and helped a young girl out. James thought she looked to be about nine years old.

'Prince James, I present my daughter, Princess Malika,' he said. Malika's large dark eyes and solemn demeanour made an impression on James.

She wore a long black *abaya* with her head covered, but she wasn't old enough to be required to cover her face. They all went to the dining tent, and the two adults sat and drank coffee while the young people drank sodas, sitting quietly as the adults discussed their plan for the day. Eventually, a servant showed Malika and her father to a guest tent where they would rest later, during the midday heat.

While they were gone the Hadj leaned close to James and whispered, 'Hafid, I will be grateful if you could look after Malika while she and her father are here. I am sorry that you cannot take part in the hunting. Prince Achmed is an old friend and I want him to enjoy his day without worry.'

In that case, thought James, *why bring the daughter? He should have left her at home with her mother.* He said nothing out loud except, 'Yes, Hadj, of course.'

'I have a small present for you, Hafid,' said Dodi. He led James back to his sleeping quarters where James found a set of traditional Saudi robes laid out on his bed.

'Put these on, Hafid, it is more suitable while our guests are with us. You will look like another Muslim prince.' He left James to don the garments and examine himself in the mirror. They added a whole new dimension to his experience of the desert, and James resolved to avoid Western dress completely while he was in Saudi Arabia.

James and Malika spent the first hour watching the hunt. James was aware of occasional surreptitious glances from Prince Achmed and Dodi. He began to wonder if his meeting with Malika was the true purpose of the day, but he put the thought aside. Eventually, bored with the falconry, they wandered across the sand a little way from the adults. Speaking in Arabic, James asked Malika about her family.

'I am surprised to find a European who can speak Arabic,' she said. 'You are the first that I have met.'

'I am surprised that you speak English with an English accent. Most people learn it with an American accent these days.'

'It was a matter of choice by my parents,' she said.

Malika began to test the depth of James' knowledge of her language. She felt inclined to give him a lesson in the flora and fauna of the desert and the finer points of features such as dunes and rocks. James was comfortable in her company despite their five-year age difference. It was like entertaining one of his younger sister's friends. He had read the classic desert world novel "Dune" that year and, rather romantically, began to imagine himself as the young Muad'Dib and Malika as his wife, Chani.

'We have many sand here in Saudi Arabia,' she said, and it was James' turn to give instruction.

'Much sand, many grains of sand,' he explained.

That evening, after Malika and her father left to return to their home in Riyadh, James and the Hadj sat by the campfire. The sky turned from dark blue to a star-flecked, velvet black. 'Ah, Hafid, the fingernail of the Prophet,' said the Hadj pointing at the thin crescent Moon above them as they sat in quiet contemplation. 'Did you enjoy your day with your new friend?'

James still suspected that he and Prince Achmed had arranged the day so that he would spend time with Malika. His feelings about her were a private matter, nobody's business but his own, and he was non-committal in his answer. His grandfather noted his reserve and changed the subject, turning the conversation to the chapter of the "Seven Pillars of Wisdom" that James was reading. He knew that James found T E Lawrence's account of the Arab revolt against the Ottoman Turks fascinating. Each new chapter sparked questions and discussions between them.

'Why can't the Arab nations unite and present a common face to their enemies?' asked James. 'Surely, this has always held them back.'

The Hadj sighed, 'It must be the will of Allah,' he said. 'But what a force for peace we could be.'

James was diplomatic enough to say nothing. He remembered reading of Saladin's offer to his vanquished adversaries, 'The Book or the sword,' and knew that many had taken the sword.

Now that Malika had left the camp, James abandoned his imaginary Muad'Dib pretensions and, with his blond hair and light colouring, continued his private emulation of Lawrence of Arabia. He had seen a photograph of T E Lawrence dressed in Bedouin costume but it was Peter O'Toole's portrayal of Lawrence in the film that captivated James. Although he didn't have O'Toole's piercing blue eyes, he could still imagine himself at the head of a mounted army of tribesmen, galloping across the desert towards the Turkish lines, his white robes billowing as he shouted, 'No prisoners, no prisoners.' He pictured his army waving their curved swords in the air and shouting, 'Lawrence, Lawrence,' he had his doubts about the, 'No prisoners' part.

The Hadj sang a snatch from a song James had never heard before:

'The wind passes like a caress over the waves of the desert sand

And the caravan leaves no more trace than a bird's wing in the air or a fish in the water.'

'And remember, Hafid,' he said, 'all things will pass, and we will pass, and we will be forgotten, like the millions before us and the millions after us. But if we believe that resurrection is certain, we will find our way to the true oasis.'

James decided that this was a good moment to

ask another of his serious questions. 'What is the difference between the Sunni and the Shia, Hadji?'

The Hadj thought for a moment. 'Well Hafid, the three main branches of the tree of faith divide into smaller branches as people's beliefs differ from one another. The Christians have Catholics and Protestants, the Jews have the Ashkenazim and the Sephardim, and the Muslims have the Sunni and the Shia. There are many further subdivisions but I see the leaves on the great tree of faith as the individual believers, and the sun shining on them as the blessing of Allah, who loves us all.' Tears glistened in the corners of his eyes.

He continued, 'Sunnis and Shias lived peacefully together for centuries and often intermarried. There is no need for the strife that exists between them now. The spiritual unification of all the Muslims in the world into a united Ummah would be a great cause for good. Unification of the Ummah should be every Muslim's goal. Remember, Islam is not a group of nations which share a religion, but a religion which interfering imperialist occupiers divided into nations. The early Caliphates were unified states and lasted for hundreds of years.'

James murmured in respectful agreement and the two retired to their respective tents soon after.

***

In London and Langley, they listened to the conver-

sation and shuddered at the idea of a united Ummah of nearly two billion Muslims.

***

James and Malika met irregularly over the next few years, and Dodi and Diana encouraged them to keep in touch, so they HoloSkyped occasionally. He enjoyed the memory of her slight bossiness and her surprise at his ignorance of basic desert knowledge. Knowledge that was obvious to a nine-year-old girl who lived at the desert's edge.

They exchanged gifts on each other's birthdays. On his sixteenth birthday, James received an illustrated copy of the Rubaiyat of Omar Khayyam. Malika had marked a quotation that she liked.

"Dead yesterdays and unborn tomorrows, why fret about them if today is sweet."

James messaged her, 'I love the verses and the illustrations. The poet's advice down the ages rings true. If only life was that simple.'

One of the illustrations in the book disturbed James. It showed an old woman, dressed in rags, sitting alone at the side of a rocky road. She was wizened and leaned forward on her stick for support. James thought of his still beautiful mother Princess Isabella and knew that one day she might be old and infirm like the woman in the drawing. The thought made him melancholy, and sometimes when Isabella caught him staring at her, she would offer him, 'a penny for his thoughts' but he could never explain his feelings to her. He would shrug off her question saying he had been day-dreaming, but it was something he thought about often.

He hoped that when his mother was older, she would be like his grandmother, Princess Diana, who was still elegant and much admired, even in her late sixties. She was a fashion icon to women of her age group, and had made scarves and head coverings, "de rigueur." James couldn't imagine her sitting at the side of the road in rags and leaning on a walking stick.

CHAPTER 4

London, England: 2030

James sat in the front row of Westminster Abbey. He watched the Coronation ceremony with mixed feelings. King Charles had died several months before but his sense of loss at his Grandfather's death was offset by this joyous occasion as his father, King William, was crowned King of England. The ceremonial uniforms, the coronets, the gorgeous colours of the robes, all made for a splendid display. He was convinced that there wasn't a country in the world that could put on a pageant to match this, and it was all authentic, not just made up as it seemed to be in countries with much shorter histories. Prince James realised that, if all went to plan, in a little over twenty years' time, he would be at the centre of a similar ceremony: his father had assured him of his intention to retire when he reached the age of seventy, so James expected to succeed him as he approached the age of forty.

The ceremonies continued as King William V swore to uphold the laws of England and its Church, was anointed with holy oil, invested with the royal regalia and finally crowned by the Archbishop of Canterbury. His wife Isabella was herself anointed and crowned Queen Consort. James was glad to be out of the spotlight until he joined the royal party as it left the Cathedral. There was the customary appearance on the balcony at Buckingham Palace to get through and then a few hours rest before the banquet.

At James' suggestion, some bending of the rules of protocol allowed Princess Malika, who was a member of the Saudi royal party, to sit next to him. She was twelve years old now. He had noticed that girls seemed to mature much faster than boys. She seemed self-assured and friendly, but in a formal way. They used titles when they addressed each other in public. At the end of the meal, he whispered, 'This place is always bloody freezing, let's find somewhere warm and quiet. You can bring me up to date on what's going on in Saudi.'

Malika slipped away as did James a few minutes later. Meeting in one of the small drawing rooms towards the rear of the palace, they sat on a couch in front of an electric fire, its flame effects dancing in the low light.

'I am sorry for the loss of your grandfather, King Charles,' said Malika. 'I hope that you will not miss him too much.'

'Thank you, Malika. He was good company and very kind to his grandchildren, he was only eighty-two when he died, which is quite young in our family.'

'And now your father will be King William the Fifth. How old is he?'

'He's forty-eight,' said James.

'So, he might reign for fifty years.'

'No, not likely, he wants to retire when he's seventy, he doesn't think it's reasonable to carry on beyond that age.'

'So, you will take over and become King James?'

'I will be King James the Seventh, barring accidents.'

'And how old will you be, James?'

'I'll be thirty-nine, I hope I will be wise enough to rule my subjects by that time.'

'I think you are already wise, James. But now you can help me improve my understanding of your English culture. In the Cathedral, I saw many things I am not sure of the words for, things people wore or carried, the significance of the different parts of the ceremony. You must explain everything to me.'

'Give me an example.'

'Well, who was the woman who placed the crown upon the head of your father?'

'Oh, that was the Archbishop of Canterbury, she is the most senior member of the Church of England, apart from my father, the King.

'So, who is in charge of your Church of England, the lady imam or your father?'

'Well, God is all powerful, but on Earth the Archbishop is his representative, the Sovereign's role has been largely ceremonial for the last five hundred years.'

'Like his role with your Government?'

'Yes, just like that, he can offer advice although he has to be careful how he does it. My great grand-mother, Queen Elizabeth, was a great expert at gently influencing her Prime Ministers. She used to ask them what they thought about a subject and then coax them here and there as they ex-plained their position. I'm so glad I knew her.'

CHAPTER 5

Windsor, England: 2030

When she received Camilla's invitation to tea at Windsor Castle, Diana's first impulse was to refuse it.

'You cannot expect her to come here to Oxted,' said Dodi, 'She is still the Queen of England,'

'Queen Consort, actually,' said Diana.

Dodi sighed, 'You have to accept the situation for what it is, she has a power base, she has a history as the King's wife, and she's been known as "Queen Camilla" ever since Charles took the throne.'

'Yes, but she's not a Windsor, she's not a blood relative to William, she's not his mother.'

Dodi looked at his wife, now nearly seventy years old and still regal, still beautiful. Time had been less kind to Camilla, now in her early eighties, he thought.

***

At Windsor Castle a palace servant walked ahead of Diana at a measured pace, he escorted her to the door of Queen Camilla's sitting room, knocked and walked through. Camilla wore a simple black suit as befitted a widow in mourning, Diana wore a hijab which left her face visible and a dark floor-length robe. Diana had briefly considered wearing a niqab which would have left only her eyes visible. It would have given her an advantage: she knew that most westerners found conversation with women who had covered faces uncomfortable. Camilla played her own power game by staying seated as the servant escorted Diana to the sofa opposite hers. A low table separated them, she gestured for Diana to sit down, and waited as the servant poured the tea and then withdrew, closing the door behind him.

'Pardon me for not getting up, Dear, all that riding in my early years seems to be catching up with me. I'm overdue for operations on both hips but I keep putting them off. Anyway, you won't be interested in my ailments.' She switched on a radio that was placed in the middle of the table that separated them. Music began to play loudly, she leaned forward and whispered.

'Let's deal with the business in hand, Dear, the transfer of the power behind the throne. We have to come to an agreement about the roles we'll play in the future. Obviously, as the widow of the last King, I will assume the role of Queen Mother and take a step back in my royal duties, but what we are going to do with you, I'm at all not sure.' She reached for a silver cigarette box, opened it and offered it to Diana who shook her head impatiently. Camilla lifted out a vape.

Diana leaned forward and hissed. 'I suggest you start *packing,* Camilla.'

Camilla paused momentarily, took a small pull on her vape. 'I've already started, Dear. I will be moving into Clarence House over the next couple of weeks. William and Isabella will shortly be moving here to Windsor.'

'I suggest you cut your losses, Camilla, and send your goods and chattels straight to Highgrove. You must have some pleasant memories from when you and Charles lived there while he was still Prince of Wales.'

'Why would I want to go and live down there again, I'd be remote from the Royal Family. How would I keep in touch, how would I know what was going on?'

'The reason you're not going to Clarence House, Camilla, is that Dodi and I are moving in there.'

'Don't be ridiculous, Dear, Clarence House is the traditional residence of the Queen Mother, and that is the role that I shall fill now that Charles has passed away.'

Diana stared unblinkingly at Camilla. 'My son has been crowned King of England and I am the mother of the monarch, not you. I don't believe there is a defined role for the monarch's step-mother. No, I am the King's mother, and that is my role to play. Your time is over, and the sooner you realise it the better.'

She stood and walked towards the door which

opened, seemingly of its own volition.

***

Back at Vauxhall Cross, the headquarters of MI6, the Secret Intelligence Service, the listeners were surprised to hear the "Flight of the Valkyries" played at high volume. On their screens, they saw Camilla gesture for Diana to sit opposite her. They watched as the two women spoke, heads close together. Not even the professional lip readers could be of much help. The conversation lasted for ten minutes, after which they saw Diana leave.

'That's all I can tell you, Sir,' said the palace servant when privately questioned by the plain-clothes policeman. 'When she arrived, she was as stiff and formal as could be, but when she left, she was all smiles and, "Thank you very much."'

CHAPTER 6

Daily Mail Online: 29th September 2030

Diana the new Queen Mum moves into Clarence House. Welcome back, ma'am.

Removal trucks arrived at Clarence House today as the Fayed family moved in. A source close to the Palace said Diana and Dodi will move in permanently while their son and daughter, Faisil and Aisha will keep apartments there for when they're in London.

After the coronation of King William earlier this year, His Majesty has graciously granted Princess Diana the title of 'Queen Mother' and returned her HRH honorific which was removed when she and Charles divorced. Aged thirteen at the time, William said, 'Don't worry, Mummy, I will give it back to you one day when I am King.' And that's just what he's done.

Diana's official return to the Royal Family, after an absence of over thirty years, marks a new chapter in British public life. It has been particularly welcomed by the Muslim community who are delighted that members of their faith are so closely associated with the 'Royals'. Last week the committee and congregation of the Birmingham Central Mosque threw a huge bash for Diana and Dodi to celebrate his new title of "Duke of Birmingham."

It's "all change" for the Royals as widowed Queen Camilla retires to Highgrove House in Gloucestershire to "pursue her interest in gardening."

Sir Andy Murray, the First Minister of Scotland, will attend the second coronation of King William next month in Edinburgh Castle and will place the Crown of Scotland on the monarch's head. It's the first time it has been used since 1651 so they'll have to get the Brasso out. Sir Andy said it would be 'A secular and very Scottish ceremony.' Lots of bagpipes then Andy, let's hope His Majesty can find his earplugs.

After the ceremony, the Royal Family will travel to Balmoral Castle where they will spend a two-week holiday before returning home in England.

Since Princess Diana's official return there have been reports of strange noises emanating from the traditional burial place of the Royal Family, St James' Chapel at Windsor Castle. Apparently, several deceased family members can be heard spinning in their graves.

CHAPTER 7

Riyadh, Saudi Arabia: 2032

Malika and her parents had been watching television together in their apartment in the Erga Palace. As the programme ended Malika's father, Prince Achmed, muted the screen and turned to his daughter.

'You will be pleased to hear that your friend Prince James will be visiting us, my Dear.'

'When will he be coming, *Abba?*'

'He will arrive next week, his uncle Faisil and I have some business to attend to, and he and the Prince will be staying at the Fayed's house here in Riyadh. Perhaps you would like to entertain your friend for the afternoon. Invite him over for a swim, improve his Arabic. Your mother will be there, in the background, so to speak.'

'Do you like James, Father?'

'I like him very much, his manners are impeccable, he understands our ways. He knows how to behave, and of course, his grasp of our language and culture is impressive in a European.'

'So, you approve of our friendship, Abba?'

'I approve fully, Habibi. Just remember that you

are fourteen and on the verge of womanhood. Be a friend to James but, above all, be modest.'

A week later James and Malika sat on the edge of the pool with their legs in the water, it helped to cool them in the furnace-like heat. James was nineteen and had started his degree in Oriental studies at Oxford. He was taller than last time she'd seen him and his body had become more muscular. The atmosphere between the two had also altered subtly. They had swum together and splashed about, and were now playing their usual Arabic word games. Malika was inwardly pondering her father's instruction to be modest and wondering how to accomplish this while wearing a western style one-piece bathing costume.

She looked at her mother sitting with several friends talking and drinking juice at a nearby table, fiddling with their smartphones, and felt James' little finger stroke her hand where it rested close to his on the poolside coping. Something strange happened in the pit of her stomach. She placed a hand on his shoulder and pushed herself up.

'I must get my bathrobe, James, I don't want to catch too much sun.' James smiled up at her. 'Would you like to walk in the gardens, Your Highness?' she asked.

'I certainly would, Your Highness,' he replied. He stood up and they slipped into their flip flops and walked towards the walled gardens, their hands close but not quite touching. Malika's mother and one of her friends stood and followed them at a reasonable distance. The surreptitious photograph she had taken of the teenagers sitting together had captured the small caress and was at this moment being examined by her husband and Faisil in an office in another part of the Palace.

'Perhaps you could come and visit me in England soon,' said the Prince. 'I would love to show you Oxford, it's a wonderful old city.'

'I would like that, James,' she said. 'One day soon, I hope.'

***

Faisil looked up from the small screen that his friend Prince Achmed was holding.

'They seem to be getting on well,' he said. 'You assure me that your father, the King, is in agreement with our strategy?'

'My friend, he is fully in agreement. In fact every time I see him, he asks me how are the "*tayir al-habi*" the "lovebirds?" I can assure you that he sees our project as very important to his long-term interests.'

'His long-term interests?'

Prince Achmed turned on his sound system and as the music played whispered in Faisil's ear. 'The political climate has become even more unpredictable. The King is no longer confident that his military is completely loyal. Most of the generals are close relatives, but that is no guarantee. There are moves towards democracy and equality. Not everybody agrees with hereditary powers. Where monarchies exist in developed countries, they have little authority. Our current ruler would feel it a personal castration if a coup reduced his political control. And a coup could bring a considerably worse conclusion as far as he is concerned: the friendless wandering of the Shah of Iran when the mullahs took over his country play on his mind. He wishes to have strong family ties with the House of Windsor and to know that he would be welcomed into their fold if he had to make a hasty exit from here. He has extensive holdings in the UK: houses, hotels, utility companies, and other infrastructure.'

'Sounds like a game of Monopoly,' Faisil chuckled, but his friend failed to grasp the reference and looked mildly puzzled.

'Not a monopoly no, he doesn't own the country but his holdings are huge. He talks of becoming the King of Scotland.'

'Believe me, that isn't going to happen, Your Highness.'

'Even so, we need to make progress: until now Malika and James have played together as children, as brother and sister, but he has become a man, and she is on the threshold of womanhood. Their friendship must be encouraged to develop into something stronger, it must grow and ripen as an innocent blossom becomes a succulent fruit.

We must be the "gardeners," you and I. We must foster this relationship, water it, warm it, bring it to fruition.'

'We need them to spend some time together unsupervised,' said Faisal. The Prince said nothing so he continued. 'Malika must come and stay in England. Diana, my mother, can be her official chaperone but something can be arranged, an opportunity for the "love birds" to be alone.'

***

Later, after James had gone, Prince Achmed spoke to his daughter.

'Do you remember, Habibi, when your Mother and I took you to Istanbul on holiday? You were ten years old, just a child. We stood on the steps of the New Mosque and looked towards the Galata Bridge spanning the waters that separate Europe and Asia. Darkness was falling, and we heard the *Muezzin* calling the faithful to prayer, on their way home from work.

'I remember, Father, we went into the mosque and said our evening prayers.'

'Like the Galata Bridge, you must be the bridge between the West and the East, between the House of Windsor and the House of Saud.'

Malika said nothing as she tried to understand the significance of her father's words.

'Do you remember the many fishermen standing on the bridge with their rods, trying to catch the fish that swam below in the Bosporus?'

'Yes, Father, I remember the silver reflections as they were pulled out of the water and over the parapet.'

'Like a fisherman, Malika, you must catch your Prince, it is the King's, your grandfather's wish.'

'But how will I catch him, Father?'

'You will find a way, my child.'

***

So far, the listeners at Vauxhall Cross had been unable to surveil the Erga Palace. The Saudi security services had purchased the most up to date "bug" detecting equipment, and the Palace was "swept" continually.

CHAPTER 8

Pilot Officer Mary Lee took her seat in the briefing room at RAF Waddington. She counted seven other officers, three of junior rank, in the seats alongside her. The other four were more senior and sat further back. A Group Captain she'd never met walked into the room and, after a brief pause to allow time for everybody to stand up, then went through the usual hand waving pantomime of pretending it wasn't necessary. He addressed the four junior officers who'd been directed to occupy the front seats.

'All four of you volunteered for "special ops" some weeks ago, and I'm sure you've already guessed that this is what the meeting is about. You've all qualified in your initial pilot training, in fact, you are the cream of the crop, but I have some bad news for you: there's no future in it. The next generation of fighters won't need pilots, they won't even have cockpits. The policy of our Government and that of our most important ally, the United States, is to dispense with pilots completely and go over to Onboard Artificial Intelligence. Sorry, chaps, your skills are redundant.' He paused to let the message sink in. The four young pilots glanced at each other, and there was some muttering. Mary sat with her hands in her lap and stared straight at the Group Captain.

'But it's not all bad news, there is a branch of the Service that is very much available, should you choose to accept the offer that's about to be made to you.' A logo appeared on the screen behind him. It was a stylised version of a fly with a Latin motto underneath written. Pilot Officer Fisher, who'd attended private school, translated the epithet: '*Nemo fugere melius.* None fly better.'

'Very good, Fisher, although most of the team translate it as "There are no flies on me."'

The officers behind Mary chuckled.

'You are about to be offered the opportunity to embark on a programme of training in a very secret skill. Drone piloting, but not ordinary drones. In your case, insects, fly drones.'

On the screen behind the Group Captain, a stylised image of a fly appeared. He stepped aside and synchronised his talk with the video that began to run.

'Stage one, we breed maggots from flies that have been mutated to have a slightly larger than usual thorax.' The screen showed a close-up of a group of a dozen maggots as they pulsed blindly over the floor of a container, searching for food among the sawdust. None of the pilots flinched. Mary was aware that the senior officer was watching them carefully. She'd gone fishing with a boyfriend in her early teens and was quite used to the creatures.

'Stage two, they pupate.' The scene showed a group of motionless brown pupae. Mary thought they looked slightly wider around the middle than the ones she'd seen years ago.

'While their whole structure has melted into a biological broth, we make an incision in the pupa's outer casing and slip in a small pack of quantum electronics.' On the screen, a pair of hands wearing surgical gloves performed the task. 'A smear of super glue to seal the opening, and the job's done. They're kept cool to allow a slow development and our little friends hatch out eight days later, all connected up to the electronics, and ready to be piloted around by you heroes. Any questions?'

'How do we control them?' asked Mary.

'You pilot them remotely like normal mechanical drones, you'll find out about this as soon as you start your training. Next,' he pointed at Fisher who had raised his hand.

'How expensive is the manufacturing process, Sir?'

'Well, actually, they're as cheap as chips. They'd be very expensive if we had to build them from scratch, but nature has done most of the work for us, so no point in re-inventing the wheel. You might see this as man's domestication of yet another species. We've done it before and we can do it again. Yes, Fisher?'

Fisher had raised his hand again. 'But the electronics, Sir, aren't they expensive to produce?'

'It's like anything technological, it cost a bloody fortune to design and develop the first one, but after that, it's fairly simple micro manufacturing. Probably no more complicated than the beads we all wear in our earlobes nowadays to house our software "sprites." Any more questions?' There were none. 'Right, time to meet your instructors.'

***

Even with the help of a female orderly, it had taken Mary half an hour to get into the close-fitting sensuit that would give her feedback from her host and mimic the sensation of flight. Now she walked out of the changing room and approached the black couch that was to be her "cockpit." She lay down, and the orderly guided Mary's hands to the sticky sensor depressions and then waited to place the visor over her face. Her instructor was to be Flight Lieutenant Peter Hanson. They already knew each other slightly, although Mary had never been clear what his job was. She knew he was a drone pilot, but she'd always assumed it was the conventional sort. He was already encased in his suit. He walked over to her couch and smiled. She'd found him a friendly type when their paths had crossed in the Officers' Mess.

'You are going to love this, Mary. The integration is almost one hundred percent, when you're wearing the suit and visor, you'll *be* the fly.'

'I imagine it'll be like riding a horse,' she said.

'No, I've done that, the association is much closer, more like being a centaur, part horse, part human, but one entity. Once you get used to interpreting the sensuit signals on various parts of your body you'll have the impression of flight without being surrounded by noisy machinery. There are all sorts of things you can do with the visor and the drone's onboard cameras in terms of image enhancement, heat sensing, telescopic and microscopic augmentation. The only thing to watch out for is the olfactory feedback. Unfortunately, flies are attracted to things that we're not. You can reprogram your end of the interface to substitute, say, the smell of roses for the smell of rotting meat. But in case of accident it's probably best not to eat before your first few flights, the technicians hate having to clean puke out of the visors.'

Hanson walked over to his own couch and lay down. His orderly closed the Velcro straps at his wrists and ankles. 'We need to be restrained in case there's feedback through the signal filters, you don't want to start "acting out," trying to fly around the room. Later we'll show you some amusing video clips of that sort of thing happening. You'll be pleased to know that a younger version of myself stars in one of them,' he chuckled.

Mary lay back as her orderly placed a visor over her face. There was a moment of interference before it cleared and showed a scene she didn't recognise. Her software sprite spoke in her ear.

'New handshake with local CPU Westinghouse Electronics quantum control processor FD120 – 2034/09/07/15.'

'That's just your couch ID, Mary,' said Hanson. 'Tick the "Don't tell me this again" box next time.'

Mary was struck by the panoramic vision the fly had: as a human, she was used to the forward vision of a hunter but now, as a fly, she had the all-around vision of the hunted. It was strange not to have to move her head in order to look behind; she felt the movement of her host as it fed on sugar water.

'What am I looking at?' she asked.

'The inside of the insectary that your host currently lives in. Perhaps you'd like to set a default alternative to the smell of their food, they prefer it to be rotten, although they like nectar too.'

'Not yet,' said Mary, 'it's not so bad. Where is the insectary?'

'Well, this one's on the base, just around the corner from here, but the drones can be released anywhere in the world, as long as we have satellite coverage for our control link. We have a team of technicians who look after our little friends. Officially they're called "Wranglers" but everyone calls them "Maggots."'

'How am I supposed to deal with six legs and a pair of wings?' she asked.

'You don't have to, any more than you would

control the four legs of a horse if you were riding one. Most of your inputs come from manipula-
tions of your fingers and thumbs. Think of what a
concert pianist can do with eight fingers and two
thumbs. You have much more refined control than
pulling a joystick around and pushing a throttle.
Right, let's make a start, pre-flight checks first,
then we can try straight and level flight, followed
by stall turns. Only joking, Mary, we'll try walking
first.'

***

Mary's training went well for the eight weeks it
took to gain her "Wings." There was a formal passing out parade, with no guests invited, and then a
"bash" in the Officers' Mess, which left Mary hung
over the next day. Nevertheless, she appeared in
her boss's office at 08.30 hours, as ordered, to find
out what her new role would be. She stepped up to
his desk and saluted.

'Well, Mary,' said the Group Captain. 'You knew
your mission would be clandestine.'

Mary stood to attention; he hadn't put her at
ease. She nodded. 'Yes, Sir.'

'You've been assigned to the royal protection
team. Specifically, you will be a member of a
group whose task it is to watch Prince James
twenty-four seven and report back.

'Are we there to protect him or to spy on him,
Sir?'

'You're there to observe and report back. It

would probably be a little difficult to protect him, given your manifestation as a fly. Don't you think?'

'Yes, Sir, I'm sure you're right, Sir.'

And so, Mary's career in royal protection began.

CHAPTER 9

The Easter break was about to start. In his rooms at Oxford, James had shaved, showered and was looking forward to seeing Malika again. He was up to date with his essays, although he suspected that his tutors found him academically rather pedestrian. An upper second would be perfectly acceptable, one had to balance work with play. He wondered if the police protection team that surrounded him would be sitting exams. "Spot the Detective," was a popular game with the student body. James himself wasn't certain who were real students and who were part of the protection team. He assumed that the rooms on either side of him in the College were occupied by royal protection officers, although this had never been admitted.

Malika had come over for a shopping trip and was staying with the Hadj and Diana at Clarence House. Now that she was fifteen the opportunity to wander at will through Harrods and the other big London stores in western dress would be a huge treat. James gave a final brush to his hair, locked his room and climbed down the awkward, winding, medieval staircase to the ground floor of Somerville College. He pushed through the ancient, nail-studded front door and walked down the gravel path to the porters' lodge. Malika had just arrived and was waiting for him, chatting over the counter to one of the porters. She was dressed in western style: white shorts, sandals and a short-sleeved pink and white striped tee shirt, and although she was a little too young, she could have passed as a first-year student. Her female bodyguard was sitting quietly in a corner, a middle-aged woman in conservative western dress, blending into the background. The bodyguard left the lodge when James arrived and joined the two men in the car outside.

James and Malika stood looking at each other, neither was sure what to say. James took the initiative and stepped forward. He took her hand and kissed her on either cheek.

'So good to see you again, Malika. At last, I have a chance to show you around Oxford,' he said.

'I feel like Lyra in "His Dark Materials,"' she said looking around.

'Well I'm not Lord Asriel, but you can save me from drinking poison if you like.' They both chuckled as he led her out of the College and onto Woodstock Road. His two-seater drew up, the Plexiglass bubble hinged open and they climbed in. He muttered, 'Car, Bodleian Library.' The Aston Martin purred and moved off, leaving the bodyguards whose car was pointing in the wrong direction to follow as they might.

'Well, what a day I have planned: Blenheim Palace, the Botanic Gardens, lunch at the Bookbinders, then the Sheldonian, Christ Church Cathedral and a walk along Thames Path. Splendid.'

She looked out at the ancient city as the car drove them through its jumbled streets. 'So closed in, everything is so old and untidy,' she laughed. 'At home, it is all new and made of stainless steel and glass, or else there are the open, endless dunes and the whisper of the wind blowing over them. Such a contrast.'

'I'm so impressed with your accent,' he said. 'I remember you giving me Arabic lessons when we first met, in the desert, but somehow, I don't think I'll be returning the favour now. You sound as if you come from this country.'

'All a matter of having the finest private tuition, my dear, not that you'd know anything about that, coming from a humble background like yours.' They both laughed.

Malika found Oxford fascinating and, from when James helped her across a road, they held hands a lot of the time. The bodyguards were ever present, taking it in turns to walk one ahead, and one behind, with another following in their armoured limousine.

As they finished their walk along the Thames Path at Abingdon, James turned to Malika. 'I've been invited to dinner with you and the Fayeds. We could drive to Clarence House together, it'll only take an hour or so, then my car can bring me back to Oxford later. Or would you prefer the company of your *Hashishins*.'

Malika laughed, 'Don't call them that, they won't like it. They are soldiers, not "assassins" and don't use an English plural on an Arabic word. The plural is "Hashisheen."'

James laughed. *The same bossy Malika*, he thought.

They reached the Nag's Head, where the Prince's car had parked itself, and climbed in. With a small spray of gravel, it set off towards London, followed by the three ineludible Saudi security operatives in their larger transport.

Clarence House was quiet when they arrived. It was a Sunday, Hadj Dodi was at Barrow Green Court and due back that evening. The office staff were absent and most of the domestics were off duty. Diana met James and Malika in the entrance hall.

'I'm so sorry, but I can't join you for dinner tonight. Dodi has had a fall from one of his horses, and I must go down to Surrey to see that he's all right.'

'Nothing serious I hope, Grandmother,' said James.

'No, I've spoken to him. It's nothing to worry about, but the man is nearly eighty years old.

What does he think he's doing riding around on horses? It really is too bad. Cook will serve you dinner in the small dining room on the first floor. I hope to see you later.' She arranged a scarf over her head as she left the House, closely followed by her maid, who wore a black hijab.

The two male bodyguards made a sweep of the ground floor while the female member of the team sat in the hallway to guard the entrance door. Satisfied that all was locked and secure, they made their way to their quarters.

James and Malika walked up the wide staircase and then on to the dining room. Cook served the meal and then retired to clear up in the kitchen.

'Do you think I might try a small glass of wine, James?' asked Malika.

'Have you had alcohol before?' he asked.

'Of course,' she lied, 'many times.'

'Really?' His tone was dubious, but he poured her a small glass.

James' phone rang; it was Diana. They spoke for a few minutes before he hung up.

'The Hadj is fine,' he said, 'but Diana and Dodi are staying down at Oxted and driving back tomorrow morning. Granny wants me to stay and keep you company.' He poured more wine into Malika's glass.

"Are you trying to seduce me, Mrs Robinson?" she asked, in a passable imitation of Dustin Hoffman. They both laughed, "The Graduate" was an old film they both liked, mainly because of the music.

'You don't look a bit like Dustin Hoffman,' he said as he stood and helped her up. They took their drinks into the drawing room. The lights were off and James led her to the French windows which overlooked the formal garden.

'I love the planting down there,' he said, 'my father designed it in memory of Queen Elizabeth, my great-grandmother.' They stood together holding hands, looking out of the window, and moments later, six years after they first met, they finally kissed.

CHAPTER 10

Sandhurst, England: 2034

James lay on the narrow bed in his barrack room at the Royal Military Academy Sandhurst.

'Knackered is the word that springs to mind, Darling. A whole morning of physical training and square bashing then lectures all afternoon. Actually, I've got a bit of a cold, the doc wants me to take a couple of days off, but it'll be held against me if I do. Better to soldier on.'

'I'm sorry to hear you're not well. What were you studying, Habibi?' Malika's image wavered momentarily; the satellite link was a little weak.

'"Leadership by Expanding Character," is what it says on the syllabus, tomorrow afternoon they'll be "Expanding Intellect and Professional Competences."'

'Oh dear, James, I hope you feel better soon.'

They lapsed into Arabic, knowing it offered no extra privacy from secret listeners but James liked the practice and the language suited the serious subject they'd been discussing for some time.

'I still think that Islam is the natural successor to Christianity,' she said, 'And it is simple, we pray directly to God without the intervention of priests or bishops or saints. Our duties consist of only five simple rules: Belief, Worship, Fasting, Almsgiving and Pilgrimage. You already do most of these things, Habibi. Becoming a Muslim would not conflict with anything you believe in now. You could convert secretly.'

'It would be a bit difficult to attend public functions during Ramadan if there was food or drink involved. The press would be onto it like a shot. Anyway, what would I have to do, I assume it would take a lot of studying. I expect there are tests.'

'All you have to do is to say, "There is no true god but God, and Muhammad is the Messenger of God." This is our *Shahada,* and if it is said with conviction and understanding of its meaning, then you would be a Muslim.'

'It's a momentous decision, Malika. It would have a massive effect on the English monarchy. It would be as disruptive as when Edward VIII abdicated. I'll really have to think about it.'

Malika knew better than to back James into a corner and changed the subject. 'So, tell me, Habib, what are the plans when you finish your officer training? Do you know which regiment you will join?'

'They'll probably want me to do a few years in each of the services, but I expect I'll start with the Army. I'm hoping it'll be the Blues and Royals.

They get the best of both worlds: the parade and ceremonial duties wearing fantastic uniforms, but operationally they're an armoured reconnaissance unit, so lots of action and lots of racing around in fast vehicles. I'd have the rank of cornet rather than sub-lieutenant, I can't wait.'

Malika pretended interest and even managed to ask a few military-related questions. She felt she'd done enough on the conversion front for one day.

***

The secret listeners made their report to Sir Alex Finch, the Chair of the Joint Intelligence Committee and he called his boss, the Cabinet Secretary, Sir Gerald Fletcher.

'This nonsense really can't be allowed to continue, Alex,' Sir Gerald leaned towards his desk camera. Sir Alex found the lunar landscape of close-up pores and skin blemishes surprisingly distasteful but it was the fuzz of superfluous hair on the tip of his nose that was the most repellent. 'He's speaking bloody Arabic, writing bloody Arabic and talking about converting to Islam. James is over twenty, he's not a rebellious teenager any more, it's time he grew up and faced his responsibilities. He's the heir to the Throne, for God's sake. What do you propose doing about this, Alex?'

'We could tempt him with another woman, film any physical encounters and send Princess Malika a copy?'

'A typical heavy-handed military approach, Alex, you'll be offering to shoot her next. Who was it said that "military intelligence" is a contradiction in terms?'

'I've no idea, Sir Gerald. I've never heard the expression.'

'What a bloody liar you are, Alex. Have a think about it, set up a committee of your cleverest new operatives, make it a project, a competition, offer promotion, offer money, do whatever it takes, but split them up. End this relationship.'

'You know, Sir, we *could* solve this situation quite easily, quite er, finally?'

'Don't think I haven't thought of it, Alex. I couldn't possibly agree to it though. We can't afford to pull the beard of the House of Saud: they own half of London and there's yet another multi-billion-pound arms deal in the offing. Don't even mention the oil shipments or their solar energy input to the Mediterranean Interconnector. What is it about Arabs and energy? Anyway, no, I couldn't countenance anything of that sort. But it would be *very* convenient.'

'Yes, Sir.'

The screen went blank.

Sir Alex wasn't a believer in subtleties when direct action could achieve the desired outcome. He'd been a Rugby Blue at Cambridge before joining the Cavalry. He left his office and walked over the Albert Embankment to the Vauxhall Pleasure Gardens. He needed a quiet place to make a call using one of his disposable phones. The call lasted less than a minute, and as it was almost lunchtime, he decided to walk across to the Tate Gallery. He fancied a look at the Turner collection, he always found it soothing. As he was crossing the Vauxhall Bridge, he threw the "burner" into the Thames.

***

Malika knew that her father was party to all her Skyped conversations with Prince James. It was a fact of life that he saw the relationship as a matter of state. He joined her in the car as it set off to Malika's school the next day.

'How is your Prince?' he asked.

'He is well, Father,' said Malika.

'And do you think you have our fish on the hook yet, Habibi?' he asked.

Malika felt herself blush. 'You must understand, Father, that he has caught me as much as I have caught him.'

'What do you mean, Daughter?'

'I mean that I love James and I want to be his wife. He is the most gentle, wonderful man and I believe that he will be a good father if God grants us children and also a great leader of his people. I want to stand at his side and make my life with him.'

Her father smiled and patted her hand. 'You are young but I could not be happier for you, Malika.'

After the car dropped Malika at the entrance

to the International School for Girls, it drove her father back towards the Palace. Prince Achmed phoned the King.

CHAPTER 11

Arabian Desert, near Riyadh,
Saudi Arabia: 2036

"Cadmus," his codename for the purposes of this mission, lay motionless on top of the dune. His ghillie skin made him indistinguishable from a clump of the scrubby local vegetation, which wasn't surprising considering the amount of it he'd incorporated into the surface of the garment the day before. The sun beat down, and he was grateful for the thermal system that kept the outer part of the suit at the temperature of his surroundings and made his heat signature hard to detect, while at the same time keeping the inner part cool enough to prevent him frying in the midday heat. He turned his head slightly and sipped water from the tube of his hydration pack and continued to wait. He was good at waiting; it was his job to wait. He had learned this at the Royal Marine Commando Training Centre years ago before he'd become a private contractor. When he'd waited long enough, he would squeeze the trigger and leave. The Saudi Land Forces would be onto his position within minutes but he'd be gone

A voice spoke quietly in his ear.

'Target acquired, Cadmus, stand by for imminent completion.'

The assassin chambered a self-steering round and prepared to take the shot. It was ironic that the three small deployable fins on the body of the bullet and the small pack of quantum electronics in its nose had relieved him of the need for accuracy. He'd calculated the approximate angle of inclination, although it wasn't critical, and he knew the general direction of the target, four kilometres away in an open area outside Riyadh. As long as a targeting beacon was in position, the round would lock on to it and arrive seconds after he discharged it. The customer had specified a mercury filled bullet, so he assumed it was a head shot. Old-fashioned but effective. After the bullet's casing had penetrated the victim's skull, the mercury would continue as a cloud of supersonic droplets, pulping the victim's brain. No deflections off the bone and a miraculous recovery, a binary result: life if he missed, certain death if not.

He didn't know who the target was, neither did he want to. There were other ways of getting the job done, but they all required larger, more trackable items of military hardware. He assumed that the need for deniability on the part of his customer was paramount. It was the limited range of the steerable bullet that required his presence.

'Immediate go, Cadmus.'

He fired, stood, broke down the rifle and piled

it with the other equipment he was leaving behind. He triggered the timed incendiaries. All the
evidence would be burned or cauterised a few
minutes after he'd left, there would be no specks
of DNA to trace the assassination back to him. He
jogged across the sand to the motorway two hundred metres away, where a beaten-up pickup half-
full of goats was parked on the hard shoulder. The
bonnet was up and the driver was fiddling under
it. When he saw Cadmus, he dropped the bonnet
and got into the driver's seat. Cadmus climbed
into the back, thumped the back of the cab, lay
down, and pulled the ghillie skin over himself.
The goats began to nibble at it as the truck drove
sedately away. A few minutes later, he heard the
clatter of choppers passing over, heading back in
the direction of his pitch. He'd been counting off
seconds ever since he'd triggered the incendiaries
and reckoned that they'd fire about now. He settled down and made himself as comfortable as he
could for the drive to Bahrain, several hours away.

His ride dropped him at a back-street hotel. He
left the ghillie skin and went inside. After a quick
change of clothes in his room and a taxi ride to
the airport, he boarded a commercial flight to his
home in Cyprus. A substantial deposit had already
been paid into his numbered Zurich bank account.
He wouldn't know if the mission had been a suc-
cess until he read about it on the news screens or,
if it was hushed up, when the second half of the

money arrived.

***

James and Malika walked among the mud-brick ruins of the ancient city of Al Diriyah, north-west of Riyadh. They both wore traditional dress. James felt a great urge to hold Malika's hand but it would be a cultural indiscretion as in the Arab world, only men hold hands in public.

'Hundreds of years ago this city was the capital of Saudi Arabia,' said Malika. 'The Salwa Palace over there was the home of our family in those days.'

'I love the rounded contours of the ruins,' said James, 'They're very striking.'

'Coming from somebody of your background that's quite a compliment,' said Malika.

'What do you mean?' asked James.

'Well, your family seems to own a lot of ruins of one type or another.'

James looked to see if she was being ironic, he wasn't sure, she seemed to be serious.

'I always thought it was very sensible of your father, King William, to do a degree in History of Art, given that he owns so much of it.' She laughed.

'Don't make fun of the King of England,' he said, mock seriously.

'I won't if you don't,' she chuckled. 'Would you like to visit one of the museums here or would you prefer a coffee?'

'A coffee would be nice, when can we go home

and, er, be alone?'

'Just another hour or so, Habibi, then we can go back to my quarters and rest.'

***

Mary reported for her shift at RAF Waddington as usual. She changed into her sensuit, went out to the control couches and lay down while Maureen, her orderly, coupled her up to the system in her usual efficient manner. As Maureen placed the visor over Mary's face the software finished booting up and she found herself linked to a drone in the portable insectarium of a wrangler's car near James and Malka's location. She'd done her usual preparation and knew the layout of the ruins of the ancient city of Al Diriyah on the outskirts of Riyadh. Her mission was to accompany the Royal Couple as they walked and talked among the old buildings, evidence of a previous glorious civilisation very different to Saudi Arabia's current one. She flew out of the car window and caught up with her charges. A quick scan of the area showed her that Malika's bodyguards were in position as usual. Mary flew to Malika's shoulder where her host stood, combing its legs and stroking its eyes. When possible, Mary liked to let her charges perform their ablutions, they were more tractable when they felt clean. Her sprite spoke in her ear.

'Orders from headquarters, ma'am. They want you to take up a position on the female subjects head.'

'Tell them I'm in a good spot at the moment and

I don't want to risk drone injury. Malika's carrying a fly whisk, they're de rigueur over here at the moment.'

'They want you as close to her ear as possible.'

In the background, Mary heard a faint voice.

'Target acquired Cadmus, stand by for imminent completion.'

'What was that?' she asked.

'I'm afraid I don't understand the question, ma'am.'

'That crosstalk, ask them what the "target" is that they're talking about.' There was a pause.

'They say it's unrelated, ma'am, a signals mix-up due to atmospheric conditions. They want to know if you are in position yet and if your location beacon is functional?'

'Tell them I am, and yes, it is.' Mary was suspicious of the radio traffic; she flew her drone off Malika's shoulder and circled above the couple while she thought what to do.

'Immediate go, Cadmus.' *The same faint voice.*

Though her external microphones Mary heard a loud crack, she recognised the sound of a passing bullet's shockwave, there was a thump and a cloud of dust sprang from a baked mud wall close by. She glimpsed a fist-sized hole with loose sand trickling from it. Mary's drone fought to maintain its orientation in the turbulence of the bullet's passage. *Shit, that was close,* she thought. A proximity alarm was flashing, but the warning had been simultaneous with the projectile's arrival. *A self-targeting round, locked onto me.* She wondered if there would be any more on their way and switched off her location beacon in the hope that they wouldn't be able to find her.

The sudden destruction of her drone would cause her a lot of discomfort: nausea, disorientation and possibly even physical injury if her blood pressure wasn't properly controlled. She flew to a nearby ledge and recorded the action. Through her sprite, her headquarters asked for a report but she ignored it.

Malika's bodyguards went into their well-rehearsed routine. The female guard grabbed her and threw her to the ground then lay on top of her. The other two brought their machine pistols out from under their robes and scanned the area, shouting at the scattering of tourists, who had been allowed into the ruins during the royal couple's visit. Many of them were military personnel in civilian clothes. They all lay down. One of the bodyguards spoke into his wrist radio. Mary heard the word 'helicopter.'

James' personal protection officer had rugby-tackled him to the ground, produced an automatic pistol and crouched, scanning the area while pushing the Prince in the small of his back and saying, 'Stay down, Sir, stay where you are.'

The PO had been accompanying Prince James for a couple of years and they seemed quite friendly. Mary hadn't seen him in "action mode" before, she was impressed despite her previous judgement of him as a rather effete private schoolboy. He continued to press James to the ground until a chopper arrived, bristling with dangerous looking, black-clad Saudi Special Forces. They deployed from the landing skids before the craft had touched down, ran over and surrounded the Royal couple, dragged them to their feet before running them back to the chopper and virtually throwing them aboard. It lifted off and flew in the direction of the Erga Palace in Riyadh leaving a huge dust cloud behind.

Mary flew her host back to the wrangler's car a few hundred metres away. She left it on a sugar water pad in the portable insectarium and disengaged.

She was "back in the room" at RAF Waddington, lying on her control couch. Her orderly, Maureen, stood up from her jump seat, released the wrist and ankle straps, lifted off Mary's visor and then fussed around, disconnecting fibre optic leads from her suit. When she'd finished, Mary sat up, swung her legs off the couch, stood and walked to the changing rooms. She took off her sensuit, hung it up in the maintenance locker and dialled the cleaning cycle before heading for the shower. She stood in the warm jets massaging her scalp and thinking about the assassination attempt.

'The boss wants to see you in his office, ma'am,' said her sprite.

'Why am I not surprised?'

'I'm sorry, ma'am, I don't understand the que....'

'Tell him I'll be there as soon as I can.'

'He says he wants to speak to you right away, ma'am.'

'Ask him if I can get dressed first or would he like me to attend him wearing nothing but my forage cap? No, wait, just tell him I'm in the shower.'

'Yes, ma'am.'

Ten minutes later Mary walked into the Group Captain's office.

'What happened out there today Pilot Officer Lee? There are news reports of an attempt on Prince James' life. Apparently, he's just been evacuated from the Al Yamama Palace to a safe site.'

'I think somebody took a shot at him or Princess Malika, I'm not sure which. The bodyguards took charge and "called in the cavalry." James and Malika were flown out in the helicopter that the Special Forces team rode in on.'

'I need an immediate report attached to the video file; the Air Chief Marshall wants it on his screen within the hour.'

'Yes, Sir. Was this sanctioned, Sir?' she asked, barely able to control her anger.

'No, Pilot Officer, it certainly was not. The RAF doesn't work like that, we're not a bunch of assassins.'

Mary left and went to her desk in the drone pilots' office. She accessed the video file of her mission from the registry but found the sound-track missing from it. This hinted at in-house tampering, despite what her boss had said. She would probably never know who had ordered her to move to Malika's head. She dictated her report, keeping it brief, and without mentioning the crosstalk she'd heard. Mary realiseded she'd witnessed an assassination attempt on Malika but wanted to keep her head down. There were any number of possibilities as to who had sanctioned the hit, but one thing was certain, she didn't want to become entangled. It was all way above her pay grade.

***

A few days later, Sir Alex was, once again, attending his weekly meeting with the Cabinet Secretary.

'Terrible business, the assassination attempt, out in Saudi,' said Sir Gerald who was by default the National Security Adviser.

'Terrible, Sir Gerald, thank goodness it wasn't successful.'

'There's a terrific stink on about it, all sorts of suspicions, the Saudis are desperate to find out who was behind it. Thank God our hands are clean, Alex.' The Cabinet Secretary raised an eyebrow as he brought his teacup to his lips.

'Absolutely, Sir.'

The meeting ran its usual course and half an hour later Sir Alex left the building and, following directions from his sprite, walked across to his waiting car which had parked itself quite illegally next to the Cenotaph, the national war memorial.

Bloody AI cars are beginning to get positively cocky,

he thought to himself, *as bad as the old black cab drivers*, but he said nothing as he settled himself in the back seat. *Thank God for the slush fund*, that and the contacts he'd made during his career in the Cavalry. There were at least three cutouts between himself and the assassination attempt. What puzzled him was how the operative had missed. He was supposed to be the best in his field. Sir Alex hoped he wouldn't get his full bounty, but that was out of his hands. Better to move on, file and forget. The James and Malika thing would probably sort itself out in the course of time and he had other things to worry about. He remembered the words of one of his mentors: 'Admit nothing, deny everything and launch counterattacks.' On this occasion, he had only had to apply the first rule.

CHAPTER 12

Riyadh, Saudi Arabia: 2037

The helicopter landed in the grounds of the Erga Palace. James heard the twin turbines winding down and the noise from the blades changed as the pilot feathered them. A crewman slid back the door, James and Malika stepped down onto the closely clipped lawn and hurried from the landing area holding their head coverings. James led Malika by the arm to the safety of her parents' quarters. The apartment was empty except for the servants. The couple sat in one of the lounges and tried to make sense of the last few minutes.

'So, are we sure what happened?' asked Malika.

'The British Establishment is what happened,' said James.

'What do you mean, Habibi?'

'That shot was aimed at you, Malika, they don't approve of our relationship. They're afraid of what will happen if we marry. They're afraid of a Christian King with a Muslim wife or worse still a Muslim King and Queen. That would mean a wholesale cultural change.'

'But how do you know I was the target and not

you? It might be a Shia plot. Surely there are many possibilities.'

'My intuition tells me. I've caught snatches of conversation back at the Palace, inferences from courtiers and aides, the odd joke. Believe me, they want to split us up and this would have been the final solution. They must be desperate. From now on we have to be very careful, but at least this has helped me to make my mind up.'

'About what, James?'

'I need to speak to King Mohammed.'

***

In a private audience chamber the next day, James stood before a comfortably seated Prince Achmed and his father, King Mohammed, Malika's grandfather. Both men looked immaculate in white robes and roped headdresses, while James had dressed in the same simple *thawb* that he wore when anonymously walking the streets of old Riyadh.

The King smiled, 'What is it that you wish to speak to me about, Hafid?' he asked.

James held his open hands part way from his body, palms up as if holding the Holy Book and intoned.

'I testify, "La ilaha illa Allah, Muhammed rasoolu Allah." There is no god but God and Muhammad is the Messenger of God.' He stood silently, and stared at the King, awaiting his reaction as he slowly lowered his arms to his sides.

The King's initially immobile face burst into a beaming smile. He stood up and embraced James then kissed him on both cheeks. 'Now you are not just a Prince, you are a Muslim Prince, Hafid. Shall we tell the world?'

'A time will come, Your Highness, but this probably isn't the opportune moment.'

***

'You were not expecting this?' asked the King after James had left the audience chamber.

'I am as surprised as you, Your Majesty.' Said the Prince. 'I had no idea that my daughter had made such progress. I had not hoped for James' conversion for years, perhaps never. As the English say, "This will put the cat among the chickens."' Both men laughed.

The King clapped his hands and servants brought tea and sweet cakes to the table in front of him.

'The perfidious English, all polite smiles and good manners when they are selling arms to us, but they certainly do not want us as relatives,' said the King. 'This attempt on Malika's life illustrates the fears of the British Establishment. They are still as racist as when they had their empire.' He paused and sipped his tea. 'You have done well, my son, very well.'

'Thank you, Highness.'

'If the relationship develops into a fruitful marriage, then the offspring will be half Arab and first in line to the English throne. If you manage the situation carefully, the next generation will also marry into the House of Saud and their off-spring will be three-quarters Arab. This must be your mission, your life's quest, to join the Houses of Saud and Windsor inseparably. Saladin tried to convert the world to Islam using the sword but, *inshallah*, we will accomplish what he could not using the innocence and naivety of young love. How poetic if love conquers all, in the end.'

***

'You're sure?' asked Faisil. He and Prince Achmed had met in the palace gardens and were sitting in the shade of a group of date palms, the green fruits hanging in clusters above their heads.

'I told you, I was there, I heard him myself. He has made the *Shahada*, the testimony of faith, he has converted to Islam, the one true faith, but we must keep this a deep secret. I am under instruction from my father, the King, to tell no one but you, and he charges you to tell no one but Hadj Dodi. It will be announced when the right moment presents itself, possibly when James and Malika announce their engagement. In the meantime, his main concern is for James' safety and equally that of his granddaughter, Malika.

'James returns to his regiment next week,' said Faisil.

'My Father has spoken to friends in the British Government, notably the Ministry of Defence. He has suggested a secondment to the Royal Saudi Land Forces, for perhaps two years. In the light of the impending purchase of fifty AI piloted fighter aircraft from British Aerospace, he has every reason to expect immediate agreement. James will have his own personal protection officer, of course, but the Mabahith will have final responsibility. Both men looked at each other for a moment: the Mabahith, the Saudi secret police, had a certain reputation.

'Not only can we keep the "lovebirds" safe, but we can give every encouragement to their relationship. Who knows, by the time James returns to England, there might be talk of another Royal Wedding. How the world loves the romance of a British Royal Wedding, and the *Ummah* will have a special interest.'

Faisil was outwardly calm, but calculations were spinning through his head. His future could be enhanced a thousand-fold, he would be a close relative, advisor and friend to a Muslim King of England. The whole British Establishment would be overturned. He took his leave of the Prince. He needed to start making arrangements, firstly for office space in Riyadh. For the next two years at least, he would base himself here in Saudi Arabia with only short visits to England. He called the pilot of the Fayed jet and told him to make ready for a flight back to London, he needed to speak to the Hadj, in person.

***

'This is such an amazing piece of luck, it must be God's will,' said the Hadj. He and Faisil were walking together near the aviaries, the Hadj looked into each cage as he passed it. It had taken some persuasion on the part of Faisil to make the Hadj leave the shooting party he was hosting. The mixture of waxed cotton and tweed that Dodi was wearing gave him a rather Scottish look, thought his son. And the shooting stick was the ultimate accoutrement.

'The Palace hangers-on really have shot themselves in the foot this time,' said Dodi. 'I had no idea that Malika had manoeuvred James so far along the path of enlightenment. This assassination attempt has finally pushed him into the arms of the Prophet. They have no one to blame but themselves. If we fan the flame gently, we can burn down the House of Windsor and from its ashes will arise a new Royal Family, a Muslim Royal Family. It will be a sea change for the whole of England, nothing will ever be the same again. This will be the beginning of a new Caliphate in northern Europe.'

Faisil let the old boy run on but finally interjected. 'Would this be a good time to buy more land near Mecca? The Saudis can't refuse us anything at the moment, and there's a vast market for accommodation of the faithful at the time of the *hadj*. They would snap up even the simplest of accommodation during the holy month of *Dhu al-Hijjah*. Tented hotels might be the answer or even flat packed habitation, as long as it's air-conditioned.'

'Yes, my son. You need to set up offices, hire project managers. Buy as much land as possible. You're right, King Mohammed can hardly refuse us. After all, we're about to become close relatives.'

***

It was pure luck that Mary had been on duty when Prince James made his *Shahada*. As a drone pilot, her bosses probably saw her as little more than a technician. It wasn't her job to understand the significance of the information she was gathering, but as an intelligent and educated woman, it was inevitable that she would take an interest in her charge. She was aware of the politics of the situation. She could imagine the consternation her recording would precipitate in the Secret Intelligence Service. It would be shunted to the Senior Executive Officer who would quickly send it on up the ladder to the Chief, Sir Alex Finch. It was one thing for the heir to the throne to marry a Muslim, but you didn't need to be a genius to work out that Prince James' conversion to Islam would cause tectonic changes in British society. It might even start a revolution.

***

Sir Alex had been called to a meeting with the Cabinet Secretary at the Cabinet Briefing Rooms on Whitehall, just around the corner from Downing Street and a brisk walk from Buckingham Palace. The office was on the top floor of the classically designed building with its porticoes and statues adorning the pediment. He wasn't intimidated as he walked across the entrance hall and up the grand staircase, but even a Whitehall Mandarin of his seniority was impressed by the massive arrogant grandeur of the place. He knocked, entered his superior's office and sat down.

'I assume you've seen the latest drone footage, Sir Gerald?' he said. His superior nodded. 'Things have become even more serious, if that's possible,' said Sir Alex.

'Couldn't agree more, Alex, bloody dangerous, actually,' said Sir Gerald.

'But what if the relationship carries on? There's already talk of Princess Malika coming over to do a Master's at Oxford when she finishes at the King Saud University.'

'Fuck knows, Alex, pardon my Anglo-Saxon, but what with Prince James', secret conversion to Islam, his continuing affair with the "Princess of the Dunes," and Mrs Fayed and her brood living in Clarence House, I dread to think. We will have to bide our time and wait until James' secondment finishes. Once he comes home, we can get more radical.'

CHAPTER 13

Riyadh, Saudi Arabia: 2038

Prince James, kneeling on his prayer mat, heard a small tap at the door of his quarters in the regimental compound. The door opened and closed quietly as Malika came in, her black niqab left only her eyes visible. She was carrying a broom which she placed in a corner. She waited silently as James finished his sunset prayers. After a few minutes, he rose and walked over to her. He pushed back her head covering and kissed her. They held one another for a long moment.

'Did anybody see you arrive, Habibi?' he asked

'Well, my bodyguards know where I am, of course.

He pointed at the broom she'd left in the corner.

'What's that for?'

'Camouflage Habibi, no one notices servants. It's a face saver for everybody. They can all pretend I'm a cleaner who has come to sweep the floor rather than a princess of the House of Saud come for a tryst with her princely lover.' She fell onto the bed. 'It's so romantic. Sorry, James, I can't help being nineteen and in love with my

Muad'Dib. Tell me about your day in the desert my love.'

He sat down next to her. 'There's not much to tell, really. I directed a squadron of twelve AI piloted helicopters, we attacked an armoured supply column which was guarded by a company of Gurkhas. They're over here on loan from the British Army, we always used them as the "bad guys" in exercises back at Sandhurst.'

'So, was this real-time or virtual?'

'Real-time, lots of smoke and explosions, flashes and bangs all over the place, most gratifying. No real bullets, of course, just blanks.'

She reached out for his hands and pulled him down next to her.

'I'm sorry but I have to leave soon darling,' he said. 'There's a dining in night at the mess and Colonel Hamza doesn't tolerate tardy young officers.'

'Even if they're going to be King of England one day?'

'He doesn't show any favouritism. If anything, he's even harder on me than the others. That's been obvious since the beginning of my secondment. The other chaps call me the *Janissary*, quite witty actually.

He began changing into his mess kit and asked about her day.

'The usual: lectures, essays, tutorials, who did what to whom in Europe hundreds of years ago.'

'Any mention of my family? Anything I need to apologise for?'

'She laughed and asked, 'Which family, the Windsors or the Saxe-Coburg-Gothas?'

'Either of them, take your pick.'

'Not really, it was more about Napoleon and the Frenchies than your lot.'

'Oh well, that lets me off the hook then. When will I see you again?'

'At the reception for the President of Iceland in two days' time. I managed to get us both on the same table. Western dress, thank God.'

'See you then, Habib,' he said and kissed her. He turned to look in the mirror, adjusted his red checked headdress and left.

Malika remained seated on the bed and attended to her social media for five minutes. It wouldn't do for them to be seen leaving together. Her three bodyguards slid out of the shadows and formed up around her as she walked back to the car, the male leading, the two women following, their black robes fluttering, machine pistols held pointing downwards at their sides. The car drove them all back to the palace.

When James got back to his room two hours later, the broom was still standing in the corner. He sighed, put it outside his door and went to bed.

∗∗

Mary had finished her shift and handed over to the next pilot on the royal protection team. Sitting at her desk she worried that she was beginning to identify too strongly with James and Malika. She realised that her loyalties were divided: she thought about them even when she was off duty, and wanted to protect them from their enemies within the Establishment.

She decided to head over to the Officers' Mess, a stiff drink was called for and there might be some company to help take her mind off things. Peter Hanson might be there. If not, there was always her dating site.

CHAPTER 14

James was surprised at how quickly Malika became a proficient skier in the few days they had spent on the slopes of the Glenshee Ski Centre near the Royal Family's official residence in Scotland, Balmoral Castle. Unbeknown to James, Malika had spent several days preparing for the visit on the dry slope in Riyadh. The couple's trips back up to the top of the slopes in the ski lift hadn't presented a problem to James' personal detective who was a very competent skier. James had noticed that he seemed competent at everything from squash to snooker. It was the Saudi guards who had difficulties, they had no way of following Malika as she skied down the slopes. They hired a snowmobile and with one guard stationed at the summit and another at the foot, the third did what he could to follow the royal couple using the snowmobile.

'I feel rather sorry for them,' said James. 'They're so far out of their comfort zone, it's rather like releasing a flock of penguins in the desert.'

'Not true, Habibi, they love it. They argue about whose turn it is to drive the snowmobile. It's not that different to racing over the dunes in a four-by-four.'

The couple climbed Lochnagar, the high peak near the Balmoral Estate. By agreement with James, the bodyguards made themselves scarce, within sight but out of earshot.

'My grandfather, King Charles, wrote a story about this mountain, it was called "The Old Man of Lochnagar."'

'Really,' puffed Malika, 'What was it about?'

'It's all about taking responsibility for your actions,' said James.

They stood near the peak looking down on the scenery. Balmoral Castle looked to James like a children's toy fort. The previous night's snowfall had softened and simplified the landscape, rounding shapes and hiding many features.

'So, like the dunes,' said Malika, 'like a white desert.'

'Apart from the pine trees,' said James.

'Apart from the pine trees, Habibi,' Malika agreed laughing. James remembered a piece of advice that his father King William had given him. 'The most important quality to look for in a spouse is cheerfulness,' he'd said as they enjoyed a whisky at the end of a day's walking a couple of summers before.

'Malika, I have something to ask you.'

She remained silent, James thought she looked lovely, her ski goggles pushed up on her forehead, her black hair escaping from her beanie. Her obvious happiness made her doubly attractive. He took her hand, looked into her eyes and said, 'Will you marry me, Malika?'

She smiled. 'Aren't you supposed to go down on one knee?'

Just for a moment, James wondered about the protocol of a Prince of the House of Windsor kneeling before a Princess of the House of Saud, but he quickly pushed the thought aside. This was no time for protocol. He knelt on one knee and, still holding her hand, repeated the question.

'Yes, James, of course I will, I'd love to be your wife.'

He stood, and they kissed tenderly in the winter sunshine. The shivering photographers stationed on the peaks of the surrounding hills caught the moment with their gyro-stabilised telephoto lenses. As did the warmer operators of the news drones which hovered at the the boundaries of the estate.

Malika's face had been clearly visible to the lip readers employed by the various news agencies, and moments after she'd spoken, the banner headlines around the world read, 'She said YES!'

***

Mary's drone had become torpid in the low temperature, and she couldn't get it to fly. Its feet were hooked into the woollen fibres the Prince's black ski hat. Her external microphones had recorded the entire conversation but, by the time her shift ended and she'd disengaged from her unconscious host and detached herself from her control couch, the story was public knowledge. She walked to the changing rooms, took off her sensuit and hung it in a cleaning locker. She showered and, dressed in her working blues, went to the pilots' office to file her report. Finally, her superiors in the Secret Intelligence Service and their superiors, the politicians, would have to accept that an Arab princess was marrying into the Royal Family. There was the precedent of Prince Harry's marriage to Megan Markle in the previous generation, but none of their offspring was likely to succeed to the English Throne. Until now, the House of Windsor had been effectively European and Christian, but all that was about to change. Mary was part Chinese and had visited her grandmother in Singapore every summer when she was a child. There were all sorts of races and religions mixed together there and it just seemed to make life more interesting and colourful. She hoped the Royal Family would be able to welcome the changes that James' marriage to Malika's would bring.

CHAPTER 15

Oxted, England: 2040

'So finally, I'm going to see Mrs Fayed again,' Malika said to James as his open-topped Aston Martin drove them towards the Fayed's Oxted estate.

'Please don't call her that, Habib, it's the Establishment's way of insulting her. She's a Royal Princess and has been ever since she married my grandfather.'

'Sorry, James, only joking. I can't wait to see your grandmother again. I haven't spoken to her since I was a teenager, when I stayed with her at Clarence House. It was the first time you and I were alone together,' she sighed.

'Just be on your best behaviour and remember the purpose of our visit,' said James.

'Yes, I'm here to ask her for your hand in marriage. How romantic.'

'Not really, she already knows that we intend getting married, this is a formality. We have to tell her and the Hadj that we are going to announce our engagement, it's just good manners to tell them, now that my father has given his permission. You know what she's like if the news screens broadcast things about the Family before she's been told officially. It's a matter of diplomacy, family diplomacy.'

'Yes, my love, "dotting the i's and crossing the t's" as you say in English.'

'Quite.'

James' car dropped them at the front doors of the mansion, which were held open by two servants. The couple walked through hand in hand. The bodyguards' car pulled up as the door was closing, the three were met by the house security team and taken to the staff refreshment area where they sat in friendly conversation, drinking coffee and weighing each other up. The women sat at a separate table from the men.

***

'Phew,' said James, an hour later as the car drove them away. 'She was all charm and cheeriness. What a relief, you don't know what she's like when she doesn't approve of something. It's all fixed smiles, brittle conversation and a sudden plunge in the local temperature.' The car bumped along the half-mile drive towards the security gates.

'Yes, but two can play at that game, darling, I may be less experienced but I can be just as frosty when I have to be. What are we doing this evening? Do you have an engagement?'

'Actually, no, I'm free. We can stay in, order a takeaway and watch a film. How does that sound?'

'Marvellous, Darling. Just the way a twenty-two-year-old single woman longs to spend a Saturday night in London.' She sighed.

'Excellent,' he said, pretending not to notice her sarcastic tone. 'You choose the food, I'll choose the film.'

***

Diana and Dodi stood waving from the front steps of the Oxted mansion. The Aston Martin rounded a bend in the drive, closely followed by the bodyguards' black armoured four-by-four. They stepped back into the entrance hall, and a servant closed the doors as they walked to the library.

Dodi called, 'Nobody is to disturb us,' as he shut the door.

'I thought that went very well,' said Diana. Her husband stood at one of the long windows looking out at the garden, and addressed Diana's reflection.

'This is a matter of great satisfaction to me. I am old and may not see many more summers but we have made more progress than I ever expected, thanks to our Saudi friends.'

'Yes, wonderful progress,' said Diana. 'What a shame Camilla and Charles didn't live to see it. I wonder how they'd have felt about a Muslim Prince of the House of Windsor?'

'King William doesn't seem bothered by his son's conversion and his engagement to Malika,' said the Hadj.

'No, he's totally supportive,' said Diana. I think he rather applauds the idea of a big shakeup of the Establishment. It won't be long before he and Isabella retire, and they can sit back and enjoy watching it all from a distance.'

'I heard that William has discretely aquired Princess Margaret's old place on Mustique, "Les Jolies Eaux,"' said Dodi. 'Apparently, they want to make it their retirement home.'

'I'd love to visit them there,' said Diana.

'*Inshallah*, my Love, we will.'

CHAPTER 16

Aberdeenshire, Scotland: 2040

'James, I'm as disappointed as you are, but you must see that it would be impossible to hold a Muslim marriage service in Westminster Cathedral. There'd be riots. You'd probably start a revolution.'

Mary had flown to a candlestick on the mantlepiece in a lounge at Balmoral Castle. She could see Prince James and his father, King William, both were wearing highland dress and holding whisky tumblers, although she guessed that, since his conversion, the Prince's would contain ginger ale. King William was standing with his back to the large log fire.

'I assume you've considered alternatives?'
'Yes, we thought about using the Birmingham Mosque, at least they'd be pleased to have us,' said the Prince.
'There's no need to get sulky about it, James. You shocked the whole aristocracy and most of the country by announcing your conversion to Islam last month. I'm amazed that it didn't leak

out before the broadcast. Did you time it to coincide with Prime Minister's Questions on purpose? The PM was caught completely off-guard when the head of the Muslim Party of Britain asked him to congratulate you on your conversion to Islam. It was one of the funniest things I've seen in years. He just stood there with his mouth opening and closing, looking like a stranded fish. He didn't know a thing about the broadcast, hilarious. I've never liked him, pompous ass.'

'There were as many celebrations as there were protest demonstrations,' said the Prince.

'Yes, that's just the point,' said the King. 'You've split the country right down the middle: the Muslim community is ecstatic, while the members of the Anglican Communion are trying to work out what to do with their anger. I thought the Archbishop of Canterbury was going to have a fit when she gave her sermon last Sunday at St Paul's. She was like a Baked Alaska: all pluralism on the outside, covering the cold white fury on the inside. The Church of England will have to be disestablished before you come to the throne, James,' he said, his tone becoming irate.

'I don't see why, Father. I can understand that being a Muslim precludes me from being Head of the Church of England, but Anglicanism could still be the state religion, surely?'

'The Government will need to consult their legal advisers,' said the King. 'I have to insist you keep the wedding low key, while the country gets used to the fact that the heir to the throne is a Muslim and that the Church of England may be challenged as the state religion. Most of the public is indifferent, it's the political classes we need to worry about. Anyway, enough for now, we'll talk more later, we need to get back to our guests. Prince Achmed will be wondering where we've gone and it wouldn't do for me to upset your future in-laws.' The King's face changed from angry to affable as he stepped through the doorway.

Whatever else you think about him, the man's a true professional, thought James as he followed his father back to the gathering.

Mary flew close to Prince James as he left the room: she didn't want to be shut in when the footman closed the door behind him.

***

Al Jazeera Television Transcription Service
Programme: "Inside Story" 12/09/2040
Interviewees: Prince James Windsor and Princess Malika of Saudi Arabia
Interviewer: Pauline Dimbleby.

P: Today, here at Al Jazeera Television we are proud and privileged to have as our guests, the most famous newly engaged couple in the world, Prince James and Princess Malika. Congratulations your Royal Highnesses, and welcome to Al Jazeera.

J: Thank you, Pauline, we're both very pleased to be here.

P: So, Prince James, tell us how you and Princess Malika first met?

J: We knew each other as children. We first met through my step-grandfather, Dodi Fayed and we've been good friends ever since.

P: Tell us more about your first meeting.

J: Well, we were both very young, I was visiting Saudi Arabia, with my grandfather, Hadj Dodi. He was teaching me falconry. Dodi had invited Prince Achmed for the day and he brought his daughter Malika with him. We watched the adults for a while then wandered off. They left us to our own devices.

M: This was when we first started our mutual language lessons.

J: Yes, after the visit we kept in touch via Skype and WhatsApp and there were occasional visits between the families in London and Riyadh.

P: So, later you joined the British Army, and were posted to Saudi Arabia, Prince James.

J: Tremendous piece of luck. It was a great privilege to serve with the Royal Saudi Land Forces.

P: And you were stationed close to Riyadh, where

Malika was at University?

M: James was very busy, but we manages to spend time together.

P: There was a rumour of an attempt on your life at around that time, Princess Malika.

M: Not something that I am aware of, Pauline.

P: I see. So, the proposal, tell us about that.

M: He made me climb a mountain in the snow, Lochnagar, the one his Grandfather wrote a story about, and then he asked me to marry him. I think he must have been checking that I was healthy enough to bear him children. *Malika laughs*.

P: And you famously went down on one knee, Prince James.

J: I most certainly did, the occasion demanded it.

P: Would you say that both your families encouraged your relationship?

M: My father and grandfather are very happy for us and look forward to a close association between the Royal Houses of Windsor and Saud.

J: My father and mother have always supported our relationship. Malika and my grandmother, Diana, get on famously.

P: Can we give the viewers a peek at the engagement ring, Your Highness?

M: Certainly, it's made from Welsh gold, mined in North Wales, near Dolgellau. The diamond is from Princess Diana's collection.

P: It's lovely, an unusual colour, slightly yellow, it goes so well with the gold of the ring. Thank you. Prince James, how do you think you and Princess Malika will stand up to the worldwide scrutiny and invasion of privacy that your roles will inevitably attract?

J: I'm sure that Malika will be unbelievably good at the job, she *is* a member of a royal family, although her duties have been less public until now. So far, the members of the press have been very understanding, and I hope that in the future they will continue to differentiate between our time spent on royal duties and the private, family time that we spend together.

P: Well, let's hope that this good relationship with the press continues. Do either of you think Princess Malika's ethnicity will pose a problem of any kind? There are those in the British Government and the public at large who are said to be less than enthusiastic at the prospect of a Saudi Arabian princess joining the House of Windsor.

M: There is an element of racism in any population but fortunately, in Britain, they are a small minority. I am proud of my heritage and my religion and I think most people appreciate this. We have a lot to thank Princess Diana for, as you know. Traditional Islamic dress and modesty have been part of British fashion and culture for many years now, her conversion to Islam set a precedent that smoothed the path for us.

P: Yes, Prince James, your conversion to Islam, how do you think this will affect your eventual role as King of England?

J: I hope that I can become the Defender of all faiths, not just the Protestant Christian faith. I hope to be able to represent the full spectrum practised by the people of Britain: Judaism, Hinduism, Sikhism, Buddhism as well as Islam. All the peoples of Faith in our community.

P: A laudable aim, Your Highness, but not all your subjects seem ready to agree with you. The Church of England seems about to lose its privileged position with regard to the governance of Britain.

J: I think most people would agree that, while Britain has a Christian heritage, it now has a multi-faith society which requires a secular state that protects people's right to practise any religion, but privileges none. It so happens that I have converted to the Muslim faith but, as I've already said, I wish to defend all faiths.

P: The Anglican Church has been disestablished in Wales and Northern Ireland for many years, and there are those that argue that allowing senior bishops of the Church of England to sit in the House of Lords is undemocratic. Do you have a view on that, Prince James?

J: It's not my place to express an opinion.

P: Perhaps we should have a referendum, here in England, to separate the Church from the State?

J: I couldn't possibly comment, Pauline.

P: Moving on, Your Highness. You'll be celebrating your wedding in the Windsor Guildhall and then at the Erga Palace in Saudi Arabia?

J: That's correct, there will be a civil wedding in the UK, and then a more traditional ceremony in Riyadh.

P: And plans to start a family, Your Highnesses?

J: 'You'll be the first to know, Pauline.' *James and Malika smile at each other*.

P: Prince James, Princess Malika, thank you very much for being with us on "Inside Story."

J: It has been our pleasure, Pauline. *Malika smiles to camera*.

End

CHAPTER 17

James sat beside his wife in the Lindo Wing of St Mary's Hospital in Paddington holding the new baby in his arms. Malika was asleep, exhausted by the long labour and painkillers. She'd barely been aware during the final stages. James, sitting holding her hand, had been shocked at the frantic activity towards the end of the birth process. There were half a dozen people in the room: midwives, doctors, nurses, technicians. There was the beeping from the monitors, the mutterings from the doctors, the loud encouragements from the midwife, but now they were all gone and he was alone with his sleeping wife and tiny baby. An auxiliary came into the room with a tray of tea. She looked over his shoulder at the baby.

'Have you chosen a name yet, Your Highness?' she whispered.

'We have actually: we're going to call him Abdullah.'

'"Servant of God", what a lovely name for such an important baby.'

'Would you like to hold him for a moment?' he

passed Abdullah over.

'What a thing to tell my husband tonight, how I held the heir to the throne of England in my arms.'

Her badge showed her name was "Humaira" and James knew that she'd be telling her friends, her family and her grandchildren about this, far into the future. He was pleased to share the moment with her.

James was aware that things would never be the same for him again, now that he was a father to this perfect baby. He was amazed at the depth of emotion he felt and how beautiful the baby was, the best baby that had ever been born. His phone began to vibrate and Diana's face appeared on the screen. He picked up, 'Hello Grandmother, yes, they're both fine.'

***

Two years later Fatima was born in the same ward at St Mary's. The second birth went much more easily for Malika, but nevertheless James was relieved to see both mother and daughter come through safely.

***

Mary had perched her host on the handle of a window in King William's private office at Windsor Castle. She'd ridden in on the black agal rope of the Prince James' headdress as he'd made his way there from his offices in the East Tower. It was always safest to sit on a black background if possible, there was less chance of being swatted.

'You don't think you're taking this Lawrence of Arabia image a little too far, do you?' asked the King. James was wearing a long-sleeved cotton thobe and leather sandals.

'It's so comfortable. I got used to dressing like this when I was off-duty on secondment in Saudi and it's no more outlandish than the highland costumes we wear at Balmoral: kilts, sporrans, long woollen socks, and what about some of the military uniforms. Anyway, I don't go out in public dressed like this.'

'No, you wouldn't want to frighten the horses. What if there's a fire and you have to make a sharp exit? Oh, well, you must do as you see fit. Now, the reason I've called you here is because I want to discuss my abdication. There's no need to look so surprised, I've made no secret of my intentions, within the family, of the fact that I want to retire when I reach seventy.'

'I was hoping to have a few more years before I take on your role, Father.'

'I can understand that, James, but you are in your mid-thirties, and you'll be nearly forty by the time I leave. It'll be fine, your subjects love you, the Press loves you, Malika's face is on the cover of all the women's magazines. You can't pass a newsstand without seeing dozens of Malikas beaming at you, their eyes following you as you walk past, or so I'm told. It'll be fine.'

'Yes, but what about my conversion to Islam? Isn't that still a problem?'

'It was your choice, and anyway, your five million Muslim subjects will be ecstatic.'

'You know, Father, I didn't ask for this job, I was born into it, I didn't have a choice.'

'We all feel that at times, James, but there are advantages, it's a very interesting life, you get to meet some wonderful people.'

'But we'll have even less privacy and even more scrutiny. I wanted to spend more time as a normal family before taking on your role.'

Mary checked her readouts to make sure that the conversation was being recorded. She had every sympathy with James, even though she was part of the apparatus that watched his every move and listened to his every word. Even the Royal bedroom wasn't off-limits to the security services. This was Government policy, although Mary was pretty sure that nobody had told the Prince.

'You wouldn't consider staying on for another five years, to give us some more breathing space?'

'No, my mind is made up. I don't want to be carrying out all these duties into my dotage. At seventy I should still have some life left. I want to get out of the public eye, lie on a beach somewhere, do some scuba diving, maybe try water skiing.'

James sighed, 'I do see your point, Father. I expect I'll feel the same at your age.'

'Can I offer you some refreshment?' asked the King. Mary had noticed that it was often his way of changing the subject or bringing a meeting to a close.

'No, thanks, Father, Faisal and some of his pals are over from Saudi, and we're having a barbeque on the roof of my tower.'

'What sort of barbeque?' asked the King. Mary thought he might be angling for an invitation.

'Oh, you know, the usual, goat, rice, lemonade, that sort of thing.'

'Urgh,' said the King.

Mary noticed that James hadn't mentioned the chicken, lamb, potatoes and salads. She suspected he found his father a little stiff in the company of his Saudi friends and they'd all have to speak English in deference to the older man. *Probably a bit like having the headmaster come to the party,* she thought. She was close to the end of her shift and decided this would be a good time to let an Arabic speaking pilot take over. Mary had studied the language as a supplement to her duties, but she couldn't keep up when there were multiple conversations going on. She signalled to her orderly, Maureen, that she was about to disengage.

CHAPTER 18

Houses of Commons, Palace of Westminster,
London, England: 2050

'Early Day Motion number one thousand six hundred and twenty-nine. The House recognises the member for Barnsley East.' The Speaker looked towards the MP in question.

Dressed in a headscarf and long, dark dress, Zaneerah Zafar rose to her feet. She had been dreading this moment, knowing that MPs of almost all persuasions would shout her down. The press would mob her as she left the House. Her face would be on every news screen. She wondered if she was putting her family in danger. Her husband had given his full support but what about her children? They didn't have a say.

'Mr Speaker, I wish to propose a motion that members of the Muslim faith can voluntarily choose Sharia law to apply for certain types of dispute, in particular marriage, divorce and child welfare after divorce.'

The House erupted as MPs from both sides jumped to their feet shouting and waving for permission to speak. The Speaker regained control with some difficulty. 'Order, ORDER!' he shouted as the pandemonium subsided.

Zaneerah remained standing, she continued, 'As long as there is no conflict between Sharia and English law there is nothing to stop secular law being used to reinforce agreements made under religious law.' Many MPs were still standing, wishing to speak.

'The House recognises the member for Central Suffolk and North Ipswich.' Zaneerah sat down.

'Mr Speaker, this House cannot condone the stoning of women or the practice of female genital mutilation.' The member sat down.

Zaneerah rose from her seat. 'The motion makes no mention of stoning or female genital mutilation; English law forbids both and Islam does not mandate either.' Her two dozen colleagues, members of the Muslim Party of Britain, the men and women who had signed the motion, could do little to support her other than wave their Order Papers. She sensed the hatred and loathing of the many other MPs, and again wished that her Party had chosen somebody else to make this hopeless proposal. Its sole purpose was to draw attention to their cause, but there was no hope that Parliament would debate the motion.

The Speaker recognised another MP, and Zaneerah sat down again.

'This is the thin end of a very thick wedge, Mr Speaker. We should not be encouraging any linkage between Church and State, let alone Mosque and State.' There was laughter from all sides. 'There should be a legal separation between the two.'

Zaneerah rose again. She read the full two hundred words of the motion, but the shouting and stamping drowned out her speech.

Once she had finished, she sat down again and stared straight ahead as the near riot continued. Dozens of MPs stood waving their arms, clamouring for the right to speak. The Speaker could not regain control, and after five minutes of shouting, 'ORDER, ORDER', he called the session to a close. Most of the members left the chamber. The MPB left the building as a group, surrounding Zaneerah to protect her from the mass of reporters. The leader of the party read a prepared press release.

'...... we have no wish for Sharia law to apply to the non-Muslim majority of the population. Our next step will be to introduce a private member's bill,' he concluded.

That evening, in Buckingham Palace, Prince James and Princess Malika watched the broadcast of the scene outside the Houses of Parliament. The floatcams hovering over Oxford Street, showed tens of thousands of chanting protesters carrying flags and placards, the tattooed and shaven-headed members of the British National Party leading the protest, with various groups following behind them. Almost every denomination of the Christian church had sent dog collared representatives. Some carried cruciform placards with messages such as, "This is a Christian Country," and "No to Islam."

Attempts at control by the police failed. Containment was impossible, there were just too many people. Fights broke out between members of rival groups. A close-up shot showed a fight around a placard saying 'NO to ISLAMANIA' before the crowd dragged it down and trampled it.

The Prince muted the screen and looked at his wife. 'We must do something to help,' he said. 'All this hatred of Islam is terrible. We must find a way to bring all our people together.'

'*Inshallah* your Coronation will give an opportunity, Habibi,' said Malika.

CHAPTER 19

Cambridge, England: 2050

The next afternoon in Cambridge, Lakar Singh, the third generation of his family to run the corner shop on Pound Hill had decided to close early. It was against his better judgement, but three hours before, a pair of uniformed officers had visited and suggested that this might be the 'prudent thing to do in the light of the Sharia Riots.' Mr Singh, feeling alarmed by the shiny robotic styling of the police helmets and their other protective equipment, had raised both hands in a pacifying gesture and protested, 'But I'm a Sikh, not a Muslim.'

The smaller of the pair removed her headgear. He recognised her from his temple on Arbury Road. 'Lakar,' she said 'it won't make any difference.' They had refused his offer of a cup of tea from the pot behind the counter and left. *That's a first,* he thought, as he watched their squad car glide away.

Lakar kept the shop open, but called to his wife in the flat upstairs and told her to take the kids to her mother's house a few miles away. His shop had no shutters, so at the end of the day, he lowered the blinds, locked the entrance door and moved to the rear to begin cashing up. A brick crashed through the front window. He ran to the door, un-latched it, and pulled it open before stepping into the street. A small group of young men, hooded and masked, stood ten metres away.

'What are you doing? I'm not even a bloody Muslim,' he shouted. 'I'm a bloody Sikh.'

'You're all the same to us,' called the leader as they all began throwing missiles, rocks, half-bricks and flares, one of which fell into the cook-ing oils section and instantly set the shop ablaze.

As the group moved away to their transport and the next target on their route, Lakar lay bleeding and unconscious on the pavement. He had seen the half-brick coming and turned his head aside at the last moment. His turban had absorbed some of the impact. A dozen local people came out of their houses and clustered around him. The Fire Brigade arrived as the paramedics loaded his stretcher into the ambulance and took him away.

His wife Sara and two daughters came to see him in the hospital that evening and found him talking on the phone to their insurance company. 'What do you mean an act of God? This was the most godless act I have ever seen,' he was trem-bling and agitated.

'Calm down Lakar,' said Sara. 'It will all work out, I'll speak to them, you just rest.' She sat on the bed and took his hands in hers. Her eyes filled with tears.

He sighed and lay back. 'I'm tired,' he whispered and closed his eyes. His wife sat stroking his cheek. The bandages were untidy with his long black hair loose and falling out of their bindings, she hoped that he could wear his turban again soon; he looked so good in it. She sighed.

'Come on girls; let's leave your father to sleep. We'll see him tomorrow.'

All over the country, mosques and temples were petrol-bombed. Gangs of thugs mounted attacks on Asian shops and businesses. They smashed so many shop windows that the news screens dubbed it "Kristallnacht II." The next day, the Asian community didn't allow the attackers a second chance. With no co-ordinated plan, vigilante groups formed to guard against another attack. Sara joined the group of locals who stood outside her damaged shop. They wore sports helmets and carried sticks and lengths of plastic pipe. The police tried to discourage them, but they stood their ground, and there was no repetition of the previous day's barbaric behaviour.

CHAPTER 20

Two polished and pinstriped Englishmen walked the long, high-ceilinged corridor that led to the Prince's rooms. Sir Alex Finch had brought his Deputy, Giles Hudson, a career civil servant.

'His office looks like the oriental rug department at Harrods,' said Sir Alex.

'It certainly is colourful, Sir, a little bit of old Saudi Arabia. His time over there seems to have left a strong impression on him,' said the other.

'The man's gone positively native, it's like a scene from the Arabian fucking Nights. He keeps it so bloody hot in there, and I cannot stand mint tea: I don't mind Earl Grey, but I draw the bloody line at mint!'

'I believe it's very good for the digestion, Sir Alex.'

'You can believe whatever you like, Giles,' snapped his superior.

Saudi bodyguards flanked the doorway. Both wore suspicious expressions and impressive daggers thrust into curved sheaths at the front of their robes. They opened the doors and the civil

124

servants walked through into a large open area. The unfamiliar fragrances of the East assaulted the Englishmen's nostrils and Arabian music played quietly in the background. The Prince was sitting cross-legged on a rectangular carpet in the centre of the room, wearing, a long loose cotton robe and a red and white keffiyeh headdress, roped with a doubled black agal. His European features and colouring contrasted with those of his several Saudi religious and political advisers who sat on cushions and window seats at the edges of the room.

'Sir Alex, Mr Hudson, *as salaam alaikum*,' said the Prince.

'*Wa alaikum salaam*, Your Royal Highness,' responded the two Englishmen, more or less in unison and with their normal English accents. Both men were Arabic speakers, but they gave no clue, such are the skills of the Diplomatic Service.

'Please be seated, gentlemen,' the Prince gestured towards the carpet in front of him.

The visitors lowered themselves to the floor with some difficulty and sat cross-legged after a certain amount of puffing and adjustment of trouser creases.

'Can I offer you any refreshment, gentlemen? I'm having mint tea but if you'd prefer something else?' Both men assured him that mint tea would be fine.

The Prince poured them both small glasses of the hot, sweet, infusion from the arrangement on a low brass table at his side.

The three men sipped and discussed niceties for the requisite five minutes, before the main item on the agenda could be raised.

'Now,' said the Prince brightly, 'about my Coronation, I was thinking of the London Mosque, it's conveniently close to Regent's Park.'

***

The dispatcher at HQ called Mary away from the proceedings. She had perched her host upside down inside the shade of a desk lamp. Her sprite told her that she was needed in another part of the Castle and that a replacement operative would arrive shortly.

Mary flew out of an open window and set off for her next assignment. Behind her, a *muezzin* had stepped out on to the roof of the tower that housed the Prince's office, he began the call of the faithful to prayer. She heard the faint cries of *'Allahu Akbar'* from the loudspeakers, with her host's all-around vision she could see the white headdress and black beard of the muezzin as he keened into his microphone. Windsor Castle had never looked better, its grey stone towers immovable against the backdrop of the beautiful English countryside.

And suddenly, she was "back in the room." A swift or swallow had taken her host, and at this moment it was passing down the avian gullet. Mary lay on her couch and rode the sudden change in perception. She closed her eyes and waited until the feelings of vertigo had subsided and managed to swallow down the bile rising in her throat. Her orderly had silenced the alarm, removed her visor and pulled open the Velcro straps on her wrists and ankles. She lifted her hands and feet from the sticky sensor panels, they were shaking slightly, although the latest upgrade to the software had protected her from a lot of the trauma. Maureen gave her a bottle of water. Her seniors shouldn't order drones to fly outside in the summer when the sky was full of predators. Still, drones are cheap and time is precious, or so they told her. *And bollocks to the pilots*, she thought.

Dr Tom came and checked her over, peering into her eyes with his torch. He looked up at the readouts of her vital signs.

'You'll do, Mary,' he said and began to type up his notes. Mary swung her legs off the couch and, leaning on Maureen, walked towards the shower rooms.

***

In the Prince's office, the civil servants were reaching the limits of cross-legged comfort for occidentals. The Prince, however, through long practice, was completely at ease.

'Malika was very disappointed that we had to have a civil wedding in this country. Although the party laid on by her family, back home in Saudi Arabia made up for it.'

'Yes, Sir, I saw the broadcast,' said Sir Alex. 'It was certainly lavish, when the House of Saud spares no expense, the results are certainly impressive.' He glanced at a photograph of the Prince and his wife displayed on a wooden chest nearby. They looked imposing in their white and gold Saudi wedding outfits.

'Yes,' said the Prince, 'we had the ceremony in the Erga Palace in Riyadh. And nice though it is, the Windsor Guildhall didn't really compare. Anyway, a civil ceremony might be all right for the wedding of a prince and princess, but my subjects will expect something more regal for the coronation. Don't you agree?' He looked at the two civil servants, neither of whom seemed willing to express an opinion.

'There are various problems of protocol, Sir,' said Sir Alex. 'Because of your recent conversion to the Muslim faith, the Coronation cannot be held in Westminster Abbey. Also, it's not possible for you to hold the title of Supreme Governor of the Church of England.'

'Well, perhaps disestablishment isn't a bad idea, in the long run,' said the Prince. 'Modern democracies don't let religion get involved with government. The Americans would never stand for it, it was the main reason the pioneers went off to the New World hundreds of years ago. The French haven't allowed it since their revolution. I really don't see a problem.'

'Our worry is, Sir, that the Church of England

is open-minded in its beliefs. Far more liberal than other, more rigid religious doctrines. If it is disestablished then who knows what belief system might fill its place?' He looked around at the Prince's advisers.

One of the advisers stood and approached the Prince, his sandaled feet making little noise on the carpet. In his left hand, he held a set of amber worry beads which he told through his fingers. He whispered something in the Prince's ear and pointed to his watch.

'Yes, of course,' said the Prince. 'I'm afraid duty calls, gentlemen, perhaps you could let me know your thoughts in the near future?'

The two civil servants rose with difficulty. With a final, '*ma'a salama*, Your Highness,' they took their leave. As they walked down the corridor, away from the Prince's office, Sir Alex spoke through gritted teeth.

'You do realise, Giles, that thirty years from now we'll be crowning his son, Abdullah. King fucking Abdul that will sound just great, King Abdul the First, yes, just bloody great.'

'How can it be legal for a Muslim to succeed to the English throne, Sir Alex?'

'Well, you wouldn't think it possible, would you? But as long as the Prince can say he is "in communion with the Church of England," whatever that means, then he can be a Muslim, a Jew, or a God-forsaken atheist as far as I can tell. The Succession of the Crown Act is designed to protect the Crown from Rome, not Mecca. It says that if he has at any time, even for a moment, been a Roman Catholic, he would be "naturally dead and deemed to be dead" in terms of succession to the throne. There are a few other rather unlikely things that might exclude him, such as violating his eldest son's wife, but other than that, I see no legal hindrance to a Muslim succeeding to the throne. Nobody even considered it when they were writing the legislation, and we can't shut the stable door now without antagonising a fair proportion of the British population. God only knows what the ramifications will be when we have a Muslim king. The lefties will probably try to declare a Republic.' Sir Alex shook his head and shivered momentarily as he contemplated with horror the loss of honours, privileges and titles to himself and his class if that happened.

The two civil servants emerged from a side entrance of the building and waited for their transport. A few minutes later they watched from a distance as Prince James, Princess Malika and their children, Abdullah and Fatima, prepared to leave for a royal engagement. The Prince had changed into European clothes, while the Princess was wearing a long black abaya, her face veiled by a niqab. Only her carefully made-up eyes were visible. Sir Alex could hear the family speaking in a mixture of Arabic and English as they walked to their limousine.

'I believe their mother only speaks Arabic to

them, while their father speaks exclusively English,' said Giles.

'If only James' sister Victoria had been the first-born,' said Sir Alex, 'She hasn't converted and shows no sign of wanting to, sensible girl.'

'I wonder where they're off to next,' said Giles.

'Apparently, they're going to open a new building at a College of Further Education in Barnet. Bloody Barnet, they're welcome to it.'

As the limousine left the Palace, crowds of well-wishers and tourists clamoured at the barriers. Many of the younger women wore coverings over their faces while the older women wore colourful headscarves. All wore floor-length robes over black trousers or leggings.

'Look at that lot,' said Sir Alex. 'We could be in Cairo or bloody Riyadh, what happened to European clothing?'

'Bare midriffs, short skirts and tattoos aren't the thing anymore,' said Giles. 'Modesty is fashionable and alcohol consumption is down. HM Treasury is bleating about the loss of revenue. The other religious denominations are wetting their pants laughing at the Church of England. The joke is that the Mullahs will replace the Bishops in the House of Lords.'

'I suppose arranged marriages will be all the rage next,' snapped the senior man, gesturing towards the crowds and ignoring the other's levity.

'Not such a bad idea,' said Giles. 'The divorce statistics speak for themselves.'

'Remind me which school you went to, Giles?'

'Finchley Catholic Grammar, actually,' said Giles.

A grammar school boy, thought Sir Alex, *and a Catholic one at that, why am I not surprised?*

He turned and led the way to their car. It opened its rear doors for them as they approached and they climbed in. It set off towards the Foreign Office. Sir Alex looked out of the window as they crossed the Vauxhall Bridge and began mentally composing the comments he would add to his underling's annual evaluation report. Words such as 'subversive' and 'unreliable' sprang readily to mind. He felt heartened to think that with a few well-chosen adjectives, he would stymie Giles's prospects of further promotion and, even better, the honours he expected at the end of his career.

***

That night Sir Alex sat in his study, a larger than usual drink in his hand. He told his sprite to call the Cabinet Secretary, Sir Gerald Fletcher, on his private number. Moments later he was connected.

'I've seen the drone footage, Alex,' said Sir Gerald. 'So, he wants to be crowned in the London Mosque, does he?'

'Yes, Sir Gerald, as we suspected.'

'Well I don't know who he thinks will place the crown on his Royal head. Has he considered that?'

'I doubt it, Sir Gerald, we didn't get that far, he had another engagement, at a Further Education

College in Barnet, I believe.'

'We can't let this continue, Alex,' he said. 'The whole country is going to hell in a handcart. We need to talk to Colonel Wilson, get him over here from Langley would you.' He ended the call.

Sir Alex closed his eyes and leaned back in his chair. Action, at last, he thought. He topped up his drink. 'Call Squadron Leader Mary Lee,' he ordered his sprite. 'Set up a covert meeting during the next couple of days, whenever it suits her. Tell her not to mention it to her boss, or anybody else. Tell her to come in civilian clothes. In the meantime, get Colonel Wilson on the phone.'

CHAPTER 21

London, England: 2050

The choice of venue didn't impress Mary when she arrived at the Ram Jam charging station and sandwich bar on the A1 motorway. Coffee and doughnuts at the "Gas and Gulp," she chuckled to herself. There was only one customer, he was sitting at a corner table facing the door. He looked up as she walked in and waved her over.

Her sprite made the identification and murmured in her ear, *'His retinal patterns are a match ma'am.'*

Mary had been surprised, the day before when her sprite told her that Sir Alex Finch wanted to meet with her. She'd never met him even though he was her political boss, many levels above her Group Captain back at Waddington. He was a true-born Whitehall Mandarin. She knew that all the reports from the royal protection drone team went to his office.

'Have a seat, Squadron Leader. We can forgo the introductions. Sorry about all the mystery but something rather sensitive has come up.' The table projected a small holographic menu and took their order, moments later their coffees were served, Sir Alex picked his up, sipped it, grimaced and put it down again.

Mary said nothing and tried her coffee. It didn't taste too bad to her, but then she was used to the stuff they offered in the mess at Waddington. She expected Sir Alex was used to Civet shit coffee or something equally exclusive.

'I want you to record a meeting and I need you to deliver the recording direct to me. No duplicates and no upload to the registry, no records at all. You'll have to manage without an orderly, this is to be completely secret.'

'That's a rather unusual request, Sir.' Mary was wondering what he was involving her in. She didn't like the sound of it, it sounded suspect, possibly illegal.

Sir Alex looked down and stirred his coffee. 'Well, I'm afraid it's a "need to know" situation that we have here. I'm sure you don't expect me to explain myself to you?' He looked up, his face expressionless.

Mary realised this was a dangerous moment. 'Will you be giving me written orders, Sir?' she asked.

'No, Squadron Leader, nothing in writing, just do as you're told and don't mention this to anybody, ever.' He laid a sheet of paper on the table. 'Memorise this time and location. I'll release the drone myself at the venue.' He removed the paper and put it in his pocket.

Sir Alex rose to leave; the meeting was obviously over. As he walked towards the door, he pointed to the electric fly killer over the entrance, 'And keep away from those bloody things, don't want you getting zapped, do we?' He chuckled as he left the building.

Mary stood, and she heard the table began its cleaning cycle. *Was that a veiled threat,* she wondered. *Wanker*, she thought. Any good manager knows that you need to keep your underlings on your side. As the ancient military strategist Sun Tzu had said, "An enemy in one's own camp is more dangerous than a hundred outside it." Sir Alex had induced no loyalty in her, during their meeting, she knew he would see her as a pawn that could be sacrificed at a moment's notice. She really didn't like him, and on top of that she couldn't stand people who laughed at their own jokes.

***

The meeting in question was convened a few days later at White's Club on St James' Street in London. Several flies buzzed at the dining room windows. The drone amongst them stood still, observing and recording. Mary kept a light control over her charge, letting it attend to its wing and leg brushing. She watched as Sir Alex and his two guests lunched and chatted. She followed as they withdrew to a private lounge where they sat in buttoned leather armchairs among the fluted columns, polished mahogany and marble busts of distinguished former members, ready to enjoy a post-prandial glass or two.

Mary knew that Sir Alex Finch was the Chair of the Joint Intelligence Committee and she'd seen the Cabinet Secretary, Sir Gerald Fletcher, on the news screens. He was the UK's most senior civil servant. The third man was unknown to her, but as she listened to the conversation, it became apparent he was an American, his name was Wilson, Colonel Wilson, and he had some connection to the CIA. Mary liked his looks, he was of medium height, slim, almost rangy. He wore a light grey suit with a bootlace tie and a silver and turquoise bolo. His Southern drawl gave the impression of deep calm but his smile seemed superficial; a phrase came into her mind, "Like the silver plate on a coffin." She was fascinated but worried that she might be swimming in shark-infested waters.

'I'm sorry to have called you all the way over here at such short notice, Colonel, but we have a problem, a very sensitive problem,' said Sir Gerald. He steepled his hands and looked into the middle distance before he spoke. 'There are those of us who feel that this country, as we know it, is about to reach the end of the line. In another generation it will no longer be recognisable as the England that we hold dear, the country of our youth, the country we have made sacrifices for.'

The country of our generous index-linked pensions, thought Mary.

'The Scots breaking away forced us to give up our nuclear weapons and, consequently, we have lost much of our international influence. Our new Head of State is not a Christian and wishes to be crowned in the London Mosque, by whom, we do not know, and apparently nor does he. The civil service union is negotiating for multiple prayer breaks during the working day and an extended lunch hour for Friday prayers. There has been an Early Day Motion in Parliament calling for the introduction of Sharia Law. A significant departure from all we recognise as British. It's as if we took a wrong turn somewhere along the line.

He's been careful not to say anything incriminating so far, thought Mary.

The Cabinet Secretary leaned forward and continued, almost whispering. Mary increased the gain on her microphones. 'We are meeting here because we have to do something before the Coronation, something radical. It's not so much Islamification at the lower levels that worries us; the religious predilections of the general public are not our concern. The problem lies with the Royal Family: that old harridan Diana, Princess Malika and her scheming, Prince James, gullible and surrounded by conniving advisers. It's a very dangerous mix. After the Coronation, the Saudis will want to rule the roost. Their UK financial holdings are enormous; we risk becoming a puppet of the House of Saud. We cannot allow it. It's our duty not to allow it.' He was red in the face and had seemed close to banging the drinks table by the time he had finished. Sir Gerald sat back and appeared to regain control of his emotions.

He's just dropped himself in the shit up to his arm-pits, thought Mary. She decided to keep her own copy of the recording as insurance.

'Who do you gentlemen represent?' asked the Colonel.

'We can't discuss names,' said Sir Alex. 'I speak for a number of senior members of the Security Services and the Military.'

'And I represent a group of like-minded people in political circles at the highest level,' said Sir Gerald. 'And when I say the "highest level" that is precisely what I mean.'

The River Boys and the Posh Boys, thought Mary.

'This is beginning to sound like a coup,' said the Colonel. 'I'm not sure how I fit into this, after all, I live on the other side of the Atlantic.'

'The Islamification of the House of Windsor wouldn't be in America's interests,' said Sir Gerald. 'We are, after all, your closest ally. It would be so much more satisfactory if Princess Victoria succeeded to the throne.'

'And you'd like our help to accomplish this?' asked Wilson. The two Brits sat in silence, apparently neither could bring themselves to answer.

The Colonel excused himself, 'Coffee runs right through me these days,' he said as he stood up. Mary took the initiative and followed him into the washroom. She saw him check that there were no other occupants before taking out what was almost certainly an encrypted satellite phone. He spoke a code and his call was quickly answered.

'Hi, Boss, you'll never guess what they want, or maybe you will, they want to arrange for Princess Victoria to succeed to the Throne when King William retires. Yes, you're right, that can only happen if the current heir isn't "available" to take up the position.'

He paused and listened.

'Yes, Sir, everything's only implied, oblique references, you know how these upper-class Limeys are. Their whole perspective is blinkered, all tied up with the Royal Family, the Church of England, decorations and honours. I wouldn't piss on them if they burst into flames.'

Another pause. 'Okay, Boss, you got it, I'll come up to your office as soon as I get back to Langley.'

He hung up and re-joined the "Limeys."

CHAPTER 22

James and Malika sat in the Gold State Coach as it rumbled its way around Parliament Square and on towards Westminster Abbey.

'What a shame we couldn't be crowned in the London Mosque, as you suggested to Sir Alex. It would have been lovely,' said Malika.

'There was never a chance that we could break so far with tradition. We have to bend the rules a little at a time, test the boundaries. We want to change the course of the ship of State, not sink it.'

The carriage stopped. 'Here we are, best foot forward, darling.' They stepped out, both tried not to think about the number of people who would be watching. They walked sedately through the front doors of the Abbey and pro-gressed slowly up the aisle towards their Chairs of Estate on the high altar. Both wore crimson surcoats, and James wore the Robe of State. The lucky few hundred subjects who had been chosen or had enough influence to gain seats in the Abbey were assembled ready to watch the ceremony. As James walked down the central aisle, he noticed the clothing of the guests became more colourful the closer he got to the altar, ceremonial uniforms in place of service dress, coronets were exchanged for hats, suits morphed into robes of gorgeous colours. The orchestra and choir performed Handel's "Zadok the Priest," and James felt uplifted and anxious at the same time. He hoped Malika wasn't feeling too nervous, he was more used to making public appearances than she was. Billions of people worldwide would view the Coronation. He and Malika were centre stage in the biggest "show" he'd ever been involved in.

***

In the Erga Palace back in Riyadh the King sat with a small group of his closest advisers. He was too old to attend the coronation, so his son, Prince Achmed, was representing him. The Saudis were dressed in their usual spotless white robes and sat on plush seats and sofas in the gleamingly appointed room. One wall was in use as a news screen.

'The Archbishop of Canterbury, the most senior imam of the Church of England has always crowned the Sovereign, but his is not possible now since James has found the true faith and follows the holy path of Islam,' said the King. The ministers smiled and nodded their heads in approval.

'Listen as he makes his oath.'

***

On the screen three figures stepped before the Chairs of Estate variously attired, on the left the Chief Rabbi dressed in a black robe and black skullcap, in the centre the Archbishop of Canterbury gorgeously dressed in yellow robes and white mitre, and on the right the Senior Imam of the London Mosque wearing white robes and a white prayer hat.

The Archbishop stepped forward and intoned, 'Will you solemnly promise and swear to govern the Peoples of the Kingdom of England, Wales and Northern Ireland, and of your Possessions and other Territories to any of them belonging or pertaining, according to their respective laws and customs?'

'I solemnly promise to do so,' said James. The Archbishop stepped back. The Chief Rabbi stepped forward.

'Will you, to your power, cause law and justice, in Mercy, to be executed in all your judgements?' he intoned.

'I will,' said James. The Chief Rabbi stepped back, and the Imam stepped forward.

'Will you, to the utmost of your power, maintain the religions and Laws of the one true God? Will you to your utmost power, maintain the doctrine, worship, disciplines of the various religions of your people? And will you preserve unto their ministers all rights and privileges, as by law do or so appertain to them?'

'All this I promise to do. The things which I have here before promised, I will perform and keep. So help me God,' said James.

The Imam stepped back and, in unison, the three clerics intoned, 'We now pronounce you Defender of Faiths.'

***

Faisil sat with his family in the cinema room at the main house on the Fayed estate at Oxted and watched the screen, smiling as the Crown and Royal Regalia were brought forward. By this time the service had progressed to the point where James was kneeling on the altar at a small desk. The three clerics carefully lifted the crown and in unison intoned, 'Oh God, the Crown of the Faithful; bless, we beseech thee, and sanctify this thy servant, our King, and as thou dost this day set a crown of pure gold upon his head, so enrich his royal heart with thine abundant grace, and crown him with all princely virtues through the Lord God. Amen.' They reverently placed the crown on James' head, the guests in the Abbey cried in unison 'God Save the King.' A fanfare of trumpets sounded and the Abbey bells began to ring.

From the sound system, Faisil could just hear a gun salute begin, probably from one of the London parks. Outside the Fayed house, he heard the bell in the local village church ringing.

He sat back and sighed. 'Who'd have thought

that we could make such progress in one generation.'

His wife muttered darkly, 'They didn't include the Catholics.'

'No, that would have been asking too much, no papists there,' he laughed.

'And what about all the other religions, the Hindus, the Sikhs, the Buddhists?' she asked.

'They're not, "People of the Book," they don't believe in the one true God, my darling, monotheists only, I'm afraid.' He laughed again. Although he'd never admit it, Faisil was an atheist; his simple logic was that if there was a God, and he wanted to be worshipped, why didn't he reveal himself and cut out the middle-men: the mullahs, the priests and the rabbis.

On the screen he saw that Malika was undergoing a similar ordeal to her husband at the hands of the clerics, as she was crowned Queen Consort.

'I think this calls for a little celebration drink,' said Faisil. He stood, opened a wall cupboard and lifted out a bottle and glass.

'God will burn you,' said his black-clad wife, with obvious satisfaction.

'You have a telephone line to God?' he asked as he poured a finger of whisky into a tumbler. 'God is merciful and understands our weaknesses.' He was looking forward to seeing King James and Queen Malika waving to the crowds from the balcony of Buckingham Palace before they attended the obligatory banquet. He sighed, there was a certain satisfaction to be had from being out of the spot-light, working behind the scenes and still achieving one's aims. Faisil knew that his father would have been proud of him. He raised his glass and whispered the words, 'Dodi and Diana, wherever you are.'

'Their Highnesses will be glad when this day is over,' said Faisil's wife.

'Yes, but they have to do it all again in Scotland next week,' said Faisil.

'How can one man be king of two separate countries?' asked his wife.

'Ancient history, my love, something called "The Union of the Crowns" a law that was made five hundred years ago.'

'I am not your "Love," I am your wife. Anyway, I will never understand this country, it is old and cold and the sun is always hidden. When can I return home to my friends and family in Riyadh?'

***

Sir Alex Finch and Sir Gerald Fletcher sat watching the Coronation from armchairs, in a private room at White's Club.

'That oath, bloody cobbled together nonsense,' said Sir Gerald, pointing at the screen as he lifted a glass to his lips. 'The country will never be the same again, it's the end, Alex, the end of England. They'll have the Horseguards mounted on bloody camels next.' Both men were slightly the worse for wear having been at the Club for some hours. Sir Alex coughed and spilt his drink, he was picturing the shiny boots, the scarlet tunics and the golden helmets of the Household Cavalry mounted on a squad of disdainful, ungainly camels, spitting as they paraded along the Mall, trooping the colour. He wondered which type would be most suitable.

'One hump or two, Sir Gerald?' he chuckled quietly, his boss ignored the levity.

Both men had wined and dined splendidly, and had toasted the office of the Sovereign, if not specifically its present incumbent, whom they both detested. Now in his cups, Sir Gerald had become maudlin. Sir Alex had been expecting this, he'd seen it before and although he too had had plenty to drink, he hadn't drunk as much as his boss. But he kept his thoughts to himself; he was too well versed in the mechanics of surveillance to express his feelings. One never knew who might be listening and, more importantly, recording.

CHAPTER 23

Ngong Hills, Kenya: 2052

The state visit to Kenya, one of England's most important allies, and one with which the old country was keen to maintain military and commercial links, was going well. The Brits had poured money into the new spaceport at Kisumu. It was on the equator and an ideal site for the European Space Elevator which was currently in the planning stage. The Royal Couple had inspected the car factories around Mombasa; the hydro-electric power stations at Gtaru, Kamburu and Kindaruma, and the Army, the Navy and the Air Force of the Republic of Kenya. Now some private time was called for. This was the family's first state visit since the Coronation and James, Malika, Abdullah and Fatima were looking forward to some time alone. Negotiations with the major news services had resulted in a privacy agreement of seven days. There would always be the paparazzi flying aerial cameras outside the security perimeter, but the royal protection team's "Iron Beam" laser weapon would spot and fry them if they tried to intrude.

Helicopters of the Kenyan Air Force delivered the Royal Party to the game lodge in the Ngong Hills where they would take a few days rest and relaxation. It was sited on a hill close to an ancient elephant migratory route. The park rangers had reported that a herd would be passing nearby, the next day. Local space tourism billionaire, Thom Branson, had lent them the accommodation. He would become a Companion of Honour for his trouble in the next New Year's Honours list.

***

At RAF Waddington, England, Mary had received an update briefing from her immediate boss, the Group Captain. She walked into the drone control room examining the aerial photos and internal plans of the game lodge in Kenya on her tablet. She climbed onto her couch, lay back and placed her hands on the sensor panels, Maureen fastened the straps, fitted her visor, and then sat down on the jump seat. They were ready for another shift of royal protection.

'Okay, ma'am?' asked Maureen.

'Chocks away,' said Mary as she fitted her visor,

'*I'm afraid I don't understand the....*' said her sprite.

'Engage,' said Mary, and she was in Kenya as the local SIS drone wrangler released her host from a car in the grounds of the lodge. Mary flew close to the Royal Party as they left the helicopter and were escorted through the lodge and up to their rooms on the top floor.

Very nice, she thought. *They deserve a bit of peace and quiet after the excitement of the Coronation and then all this world travel.* Mary knew that Malika was pregnant with her third child, but she was in her early thirties and there'd been no particular problems with her first two pregnancies. Mary thought she looked a little "washed out" as she sat on the bed in the master bedroom. Her maid was unpacking Malika's clothes and hanging them in the wardrobe.

Abdullah ran into the room, excited at not having to be on his best behaviour in front of the cameras.

'When will we see the elephants, Mamma?' he asked.

'They will come tomorrow, Habibi.'

'And will we see them from the balcony,' he asked.

'No,' said his father, 'we have to drive to a lookout tower about a kilometre away.'

One of the servants knocked and told them that lunch was ready and the family went down to the dining room. Mary flew after them and positioned herself on top of a convenient picture frame. After lunch, the family decided to spend a quiet afternoon together. Malika rested in an armchair while James played with the children on the floor and then watched some cartoons with them. Mary had little to report at the end of her shift.

Next morning the Royal Family made a lazy start. Malika lay in bed dozing as James supervised the children's breakfasts. Mary looked out of the bedroom window using her onboard cameras; the fly's vision was only good for short distances. The lodge was sited on a ridge looking out over hills, some tree-covered, which stretched to a gently undulating horizon. The landscape was almost English, it was certainly green and lush. Mary had been expecting a dry, yellow, African savannah. It was raining and her sensors told her that the weather was cool.

Malika got up and found a blanket which she wrapped around herself and went down to see how breakfast was progressing.

James looked up. 'The park rangers say the herd of elephants is on its way, we need to drive to the viewing tower.'

'I'm really tired, Habib, there'll be other herds, do you mind if I rest while you take the children?'

'No problem, my Love, are you warm enough?' asked James.

'Not really,' she pulled the blanket closer around her shoulders and sat on the sofa opposite the gas fire. James knelt and fiddled with the controls. He was rewarded by a satisfying whoosh as it lit. He took the children by the hand and led them out of the room, closing the door behind him. Malika lay down, Mary thought that perhaps her third pregnancy was taking more out of her than the previous two, after all. Mary's duty was to watch James and the children, but as the door was closed, she couldn't follow them. Her best bet was to transfer to another drone and get the wrangler to release it from her car at the back of the lodge. Mary attempted to "bump out" but was surprised to find that her software was frozen. She'd never encountered this before nor had she heard of it. She was stuck, helpless. Her cameras and microphones were functioning but she couldn't move or disengage from the drone. A few moments later one of her sensors began to flash, it was signalling a build-up of carbon monoxide. The gas fire must be faulty, she watched helplessly as the level slowly built above the recommended limit and into the danger zone, the indicator was flashing red. From where her host stood, Mary could see Malika lying on the sofa, her complexion had reddened and her breathing was laboured. Mary tried everything she could to signal her orderly back at Waddington but although she was aware of her prone body on the drone control couch, she couldn't move a finger. She tried to exit her host but even the emergency disengagement software was locked. Through her cameras she watched as Malika's breathing slowed and stopped, there was nothing she could do as the minutes passed. After about half hour the system rebooted itself and she regained control. She disengaged and was back at Waddington lying on her control couch. The medical officer was sitting on the jump seat next to her and Maureen hovered anxiously in the background.

The doc was checking her vital signs on the screen above her couch.

'You were unconscious, Mary,' he said. 'We need to do a full check on you, to find out what happened.'

'You had us worried there, ma'am,' Maureen said. 'You were out of it for over half an hour. We wondered what was happening. We couldn't get you back.'

'Never mind about me. There's been a murder attempt on Queen Malika,' said Mary. 'She's been gassed. Get the security people into the lodge right away. I think she's dead.'

***

'Such an unfortunate malfunction,' said Sir Gerald, the Cabinet Secretary.

'Yes, Sir Gerald, most unfortunate,' said Sir Alex. The two were dining at White's Club in St James again. 'The gas fire's flue was blocked by some sort of bird's nest.'

'And why did the drone pilot not raise the alarm, remind me? Was her host gassed as well?'

'No, apparently flies don't have haemoglobin, so carbon monoxide doesn't affect them. It was a software malfunction, I believe,' said his underling. 'The system froze.'

'If only the drone pilot had been able to raise the alarm, they might have saved poor Queen Malika. Have the RAF been able to explain this software failure?'

'No, Sir Gerald.'

Sir Gerald forked a piece of Dover sole towards his mouth then paused. 'The drone control system is of American manufacture, I believe?'

'That's correct, Sir Gerald. It's made by Westinghouse to CIA specifications.'

Sir Alex pulled a pen from his inside pocket and wrote on a paper napkin, 'They have a backdoor into the software.' He placed it in front of his boss, Sir Gerald leaned forward and read it without comment. He looked away and continued to fork over his fish as if looking for a particularly good piece. Sir Alex crumpled up the napkin and thrust it into his jacket pocket.

'Yes,' said Sir Gerald, 'most unfortunate,' as he speared the chosen morsel.

***

'We didn't expect them to use the goddam fire until that evening. We planned to take out the whole family,' explained Colonel Wilson.

His boss, Luke Repass, was a political appointee who'd made his name as a corporate lawyer before the President had appointed him Director of the Central Intelligence Agency. He was a man who enjoyed his food and abhorred exercise. At the moment he was stressed and red-faced. Wilson didn't expect him to make old bones, but that was no use now, while Wilson was subject to Clancy's angry outbursts.

'Well, this hasn't helped, Ed, this hasn't helped at all. The Brits wanted Princess Victoria to succeed to the throne because she's an Episcopalian, unlike her towel-head brother James. They wanted the whole family taken out. Killing Queen Malika hasn't help at all. All we've done is piss off King James and left him in place, with Prince Abdullah ready to follow him. It's a clusterfuck, Colonel.'

Wilson tried to change the subject. 'Why can't they have elections like over here? Imagine if we had a hereditary presidency and the President's son took the job whether he was any good at it or not, it just doesn't make any sense. Thank God for democracy and the rule of law.'

'Yes, Colonel, that's what our job's all about, but the fact is that King James knows the British Establishment was behind Queen Malika's death, although, thank fuck, he can't prove it. I assume nothing can be traced back to us?'

'No, sir, we used three levels of cutout. Even if the contractor was tortured, he wouldn't be able to say who he was working for.'

***

Some weeks later James visited Faisil at the Fayed's Oxted estate. They walked in the gardens together.

'But how will I live without her? She was my foundation, my rock.' whispered James.

Faisil gently patted his shoulder. 'The Arabs have a saying: "You can judge a man with three things: leadership, wealth and misfortune." I think the last is the most important,' he said.

'I want to do the best for my children, Faisil. Those bastards killed Malika, they still might kill Abdullah and Fatima. I hate them, the politicians, the aristocracy, the Church, the whole lot of them, scheming, plotting, climbing over each other's backs to gain an advantage. I don't trust any of them, they're all as bad as each other.'

'Perhaps you should consider sending the children away somewhere safe. I feel sure that King Achmed would put them under his protection.'

'Do you know, Faisil, I think you're right, they'd be safe in Saudi Arabia.'

'I will make the arrangements, Your Highness.'

***

That evening Faisil HoloSkyped his friend.

'How old is Prince Abdullah?' asked King Achmed.

'He is seven years old, Your Majesty,' said Faisil.

Faisil was thinking back to his first meeting with this man, all those years ago in Jeddah. He wondered momentarily what had become of the dwarf, the oud player.

'It would be a fine thing if the next King of England was a *hafiz*,' said the King thoughtfully. 'He is the right age to begin the training. We will find a suitable *madrassa* and a personal tutor. What a gift for his subjects in England, a King who has completely memorised the glorious Koran. As the saying goes, "*What is learned in youth is carved in stone.*" In the meantime, I will arrange for him to meet some of his female cousins. *Inshallah,* when he eventually takes his place on the English throne, one of them will be at his side.

***

At the SIS building at Vauxhall Cross, Sir Alex and Sir Gerald listened to the recording of Faisil and King Achmed's conversation. Sir Gerald stood, walked to the window and stared out at the London skyline. 'I don't know about you Alex, but I can see only one way out of this.'

'And what is that, Sir Gerald?' he asked.

'We have to declare a Republic.'

The End

If you have enjoyed this book, please consider leaving a short review on Amazon.

THE CHARACTERS

Diana Fayed - Prince James' grandmother
Dodi Fayed - Diana's husband
James Windsor - Eldest son of Prince William
Victoria Windsor - James' younger sister
William Windsor - William V, future King of England
Isabella Windsor - Nee Calthorpe, wife of King William
Faisil Fayed - Son of Diana and Dodi
Aisha Fayed - Daughter of Diana and Dodi
Mary Lee - Fly drone pilot, RAF officer
Maureen Dodds - Mary Lee's orderly, RAF corporal
Flt Lt Peter Hanson - Mary's drone instructor
Cadmus - A contract assassin, name undisclosed
Charles Windsor - Charles III, King of England
Princess Malika - Future wife of Prince James
Prince Achmed - Malika's father, son of the King of Saudi Arabia
King Mohammed - King of Saudi Arabia and custodian of the holy sites
Abdullah Windsor - Son of James & Malika Windsor
Fatima Windsor - Daughter of James and Malika
Zaneerah Zafar - Member of Parliament
Giles Hudson - A senior civil servant

Sir Gerald Fletcher - Cabinet Secretary and National Security Adviser
Sir Alex Finch - Chair of the UK Joint Intelligence Committee
Colonel Ed Wilson - Senior CIA operative
Luke Repass - Head of the CIA

ARABIC WORDS AND PHRASES

Abba - Father
Abaya - Women's loose overgarment
Ahlan wa sahlan - Hello
Al-hamdu lillah - Praise be to God
Allahu Akbar - God is greater
Alrajul - Prince
Dhu al-Hijjah - The holy month when the Hadj is performed
Habibi - Darling
Hadj - The pilgrimage to Mecca or a man who has made the Hadj
Hafid - Grandson
Hafiz - A person who has memorised the Koran
Hashisheen - Assassins, users of hashish, derogatory
Imam - Worship leader in a mosque
Iftar - Fast-breaking evening meal during the holy month of Ramadan
Inshallah - God willing
Janissary - An elite corps of Christian soldiers in the Ottoman Empire
Mabahith - The secret police agency of the Presidency of Saudi Arabia
Ma'a salama - Go in peace
Madrassa - Islamic religious school

Muezzin - A man who calls the faithful to prayer

Mullah - Muslim scholar, teacher or religious leader

Oud - Lute, stringed instrument

Sadiki - Friend

Salaam alaikum - Peace be with you

Salat al-maghrib - Prayers just after sunset

Shahada - Muslim declaration of faith

Shukran - Thank you

Souk - Market

Tayir alhabi - Love birds

Thawb - Long sleeved male garment or robe

Umma - The worldwide community of Muslims

Zaeim - Boss

ACKNOWLEDGEMENTS

For their encouragement and friendship, my thanks to the members of the Halesworth Write Types group.

Special thanks to my wife, for her editing and constant support.

Thanks to The Daily Mail Online (Alternate reality version) and Wikipedia (Alternate reality version.)

AUTHOR PAGE

Roger Ley was born and educated in London and spent some of his formative years in Saudi Arabia. He worked as an engineer in the oilfields of North Africa and the North Sea then later pursued a career in higher education.

Follow him on:

Facebook
https://www.facebook.com/rogerley2/

Twitter
https://twitter.com/RogerLey1

Blog
rogerley.co.uk

Goodreads
https://www.goodreads.com/author/list/14211596.Roger_Ley

POSTSCRIPT

This story is related to my time travel novel "Chronoscape" but can be read independently.

History is an ever-branching tree of possibilities; each small change generates a new line of events. This book is a work of fiction, where I have referred to real people, there is no implication that they have spoken or behaved in the way I have written. In this reality Diana Princess of Wales and Dodi Fayed did not die in a car crash in 1997, the rest is alternative history.

Suffolk, June 2019

ALSO BY ROGER LEY

CHRONOSCAPE

A story of time travel and alternative history

Physicist, Martin Riley, has discovered a way to receive news stories from two weeks in the future but the Government steps in and cloaks the technology in secrecy. Despite Riley's warnings, politicians on both sides of the Atlantic make radical alterations to political events. The first temporal alteration saves Princess Diana, the next saves the Twin Towers, but ripples travel far ahead and disturb Earth's future civilisation. The Timestream must be realigned, but at what cost?

DEAD PEOPLE ON FACEBOOK

An anthology of speculative fiction

Most of the stories in this book were published, podcast or broadcast in the year 2018. The collection features various speculative genres: fantasy, horror, humour and science fiction; there is a little magic and one romance. It includes the ten-part serial novelette 'Steampunk Confederation,' featuring secret agents Harry Lampeter and Telford Stephenson, who are competing for the plans of the new Ironclad warship.

A HORSE IN THE MORNING

Stories from a sometimes unusual life

Norwegian call-girls, desert djinns and Berlin roof jumpers area sample of the characters that inhabit the pages of this collection. Some of the stories have been published in periodicals, including Reader's Digest, The Guardian and The Oldie, while others appear for the first time. The book is the dramatic and amusing memoir of an engineer, teacher, and failed astronaut recounted with quirky British humour.